9-11-68

To Dad —

A sneaky way to get a rest, hope it doesn't last too long, though.

With love,
Jimmie Dykes Nolan
and all the grand kiddies

10⁰⁰

YOU CAN'T STEAL
FIRST BASE

You Can't Steal First Base

By JIMMIE DYKES

AND

CHARLES O. DEXTER

J. B. LIPPINCOTT COMPANY

PHILADELPHIA AND NEW YORK

Publisher's Note

No ONE likes to talk more than Jimmie Dykes, the
man with a thousand stories, all about baseball. With
the cheerful bounce which won him a million friends
during his fifty years on the diamond he told the story
of his life to a tape recorder over a table in the Bala
Golf Club's dining room in sixteen uncut, uncensored,
inside sessions. *You Can't Steal First Base* is the result, a history of the national sport as eye-witnessed by
Jimmie, sandlot star, minor-league whiz, star third
sacker of the champion Philadelphia Athletics, longtime manager, coach, umpire baiter, kidder and nice
guy. They're all talked about: Ruth, Cobb, Speaker,
Foxx, Grove, Cochrane, Connie Mack, the great ones.
And also the not so great, the clowns, the drinkers, the
skirt-chasers. Not to mention the big shots—the com-
missioners, league presidents, club owners, general
managers—that Jimmie encountered on his way.

Charlie Dexter, the veteran baseball writer, listened,
assembled, and put Jimmie's chatter to paper for this
fun book with its serious overtones, wisdom, and sentimental love for the game.

Contents

SIT DOWN, PAL . . .

I can't keep a secret. I'm the gabby type that's talked my way through fifty-odd years of baseball life. I've talked to owners, general managers, managers, players, umpires, newspapermen and thousands of fans, to everyone within hearing distance of my voice. I've talked so violently to umpires that I sent a bunch of signed checks to the league office with instructions to fill in the amounts whenever I was fined. I feel like talking to you now. Give me a cigar, a bottle of beer and a rocking chair, and draw up a chair for yourself. I'll tell you about my fifty years, with the umpires I've cussed at, the laughs, the heartaches, the thrills of my big days and the chills of my small.

All set?

Okay.

Let's play ball . . .

1

THIS IS HOW IT WAS

I WAS BORN into baseball in 1896. Six months later my Scottish father moved me into Preston, on the wrong side of the tracks on Philadelphia's Main Line. Dad had never played ball, he was an engineer at Bryn Mawr College, but he was nuts about the game. He'd hide quarters under the carpet on the stairs so he could sneak out without my mother knowing he was squandering the family fortune on bleacher tickets. He put a baseball in my hands before they were big enough to hold on to it and was playing catch with me by the time I was five.

Every boy played ball in those turn-of-the-century

days. Every town and crossroads on the Main Line had
a team. It was a world in which I had no worries except
learning how to hit, run, and throw good enough to
make a big boys' team. I was a catcher in high school,
but my father insisted that I switch to the infield because I was smallish and quick on my feet. At seventeen I was playing on the semipro Penn Street Boys'
Club team which my father had helped form. It was
baseball for me all spring and summer, an adventurous
life in which my idols were the great men who starred
on the Phillies and Athletics. I was the cockiest kid
around, an inveterate talker. I set my heart on getting
a tryout with the Athletics, who'd been winning pennants since I was big enough to swing a bat.

One day in Seaford, Delaware, where I was playing
third base on the town team, two big-league scouts
watched the game. Mike Drennan, the Athletics' ace
talent hunter, turned to Joe Sugden of the St. Louis
Browns. "How do you like that kid on third, Joe?"

"He's got a good pair of hands and a strong arm, but
he'll never make it. Take a look at the size of that
fanny!"

It was true. . . . I was never the svelte type, not even
in my teens.

But Drennan must have turned in a good report on
me. A few days later I received an invitation to a try-
out on the Athletics' home grounds, Shibe Park.

The following morning I took the hour-and-a-half
ride to Shibe Park—three trolleys, a nickel each—
armed with a glove, spiked shoes, and high hopes. Real
live big-leaguers were practising on the diamond. They
ignored me. I finally located Ira Thomas, the Athletics'
star catcher during these championship years, to whom
I'd been told to report.

"Go out and shag a few," he said.

For an hour Thomas hit ground balls to me. I scooped them up at my left, right and center until I was dead on my feet and muffed a few. With that cockiness I was supposed to have I yelled, "Hey, Thomas, ain't you decided yet whether I can go get 'em?"

"Stay in there, kid!" he yelled and hit a line drive through my legs.

"I've had enough!" I spat and started to walk off the field.

A tall, lean man in a street suit, a hard collar about his neck, beckoned to me. "Let's see how you hit," he said.

I did a fast double-take and nearly folded. He was none other than Connie Mack, the genius who'd led the Athletics to all those pennants, Philadelphia's greatest man since William Penn.

In those days a rookie wasn't given the time of day by veterans. "Get away from there!" snapped a player as I went to the dugout for a bat. Other bats were lying on the ground. Mr. Mack picked up one and handed it to me.

Batting practice was on in the cage. I didn't know that five licks was all I was supposed to take. I took ten and connected with the ball about three times. A player growled at me and shoved me aside. I looked around for Mr. Mack. He wasn't there. I lost my temper. I stalked off the field and out of Shibe Park, leaving my glove behind. The Athletics were not for me!

I was still seething on Saturday morning as I returned to Shibé Park in the hope of finding my glove. The clubhouse attendant gave it to me. "You're young

Dykes, ain't you?" he asked. "Well, Mr. Mack wants to see you."

"I ain't got the time," I said, and walked out again, heading for Camden, where I was scheduled to play that afternoon.

That fall I received a handwritten letter from Mr. Mack, inviting me to visit him at his home. I slicked up, shoes polished, hair parted in the middle, and set forth.

Connie Mack was unlike other baseball men of that rough-and-ready day. He was soft-spoken, courteous, and quickly put me at ease in his comfortable, old-fashioned house. He didn't flatter me; he questioned me about my background, my experience. Then, like a loving uncle to an impetuous nephew, he offered me sound advice: "You have good tools, Jimmie, but you need instruction in hitting. Keep at it, plug away, and you'll make it one of these days." The pause that followed seemed the longest of my life. "I can send you to Gettysburg in the Blue Ridge League next spring," he said; "that is, if you'll go."

Would I go? Hellfire and brimstone couldn't have stopped me. I'd have lived on Moxie and hot dogs and slept in a drafty hall bedroom to be a pro.

Note this: I got no bonus, not one thin dime for signing. Not even the carfare to Shibe Park for my try-out. My contract called for $100 a month—$70 from the Gettysburg club, $30 from the Athletics. I reported to Gettysburg the first week in May of 1917 and played second, short and third for one month.

Payday came and went. No dough. I was living in a hotel owned by a shareholder in the club who didn't press me for rent and who allowed me to sign chits for meals. By the fifteenth I had about one buck and change left from the pocket money my father had given me. And my teammates were as flat as I.

Payless June passed. One morning in early July we players held a meeting. I orated like a fiery Bolshevik and was delegated to tell the business manager that we would not play that afternoon's game unless we were paid. I reminded him that the club was owned by town merchants and bank directors who either had to come across or no game today.

"I'll see what I can do," he promised. By game time he told me that the moneybags were out week-ending. The strike began.

The father of a teammate worked for the Athletics. "I'm going to Hagerstown to pick up a few dollars playing ball tomorrow," he said. "Come on along, Jim."

He paid my bus fare and we were in Hagerstown before dark, putting up in a one-buck-a-night hotel. After church on Sunday morning we went to the ball park and found Earl Mack, Connie's son, looking for us. "Had your breakfast yet, boys?" he asked.

"No," I said.

He slipped us five dollars apiece. That afternoon we played on the Hanover semipro nine against Hagerstown, earning another five bucks. Earl Mack gave us ten more and told us to rejoin the Gettysburg squad at Martinsburg on Monday where we'd get the rest of our back pay.

The strike ended. The season ran until Labor Day. We players went to our homes on borrowed money— not one more penny came our way from the Gettysburg club. But for my father's occasional remittances and that $30 a month from the Athletics I'd have starved.

Such was my initiation into organized baseball in 1917.

Yet I bounced back to Preston on a wave of optimism. What if I'd lost money on the season? I'd polished my fielding, extended my range, improved my footwork on double plays. Mr. Mack had been right about my hitting, a mere .217 for the season. But I was a pro, looked up to by my old semipro and amateur pals, my Preston neighbors, and my adoring dad.

Then came the topper: I received a letter from the National Association of Minor Leagues, notifying me that Gettysburg had overpaid me and that I owed them money. I took it to Mike Drennan. "Forget it," he said. "They're nuts!"

I forgot everything but my name when the postman brought me a letter from the Athletics. I sliced it open: "You are ordered to report to our camp in Jacksonville, Florida, on March 1, 1918." I bellowed with joy.

That spring my long association with the Athletics began. And with Connie Mack.

Mr. Mack was my tutor, my friend, and my personal hero through the years. I was but one of the many among the revolving-door, here-today-gone-tomorrow tailenders in camp, one of the three he retained until, in 1928, we became pennant contenders and, one year later, champions. The others were Ed Rommel, the tall, lean knuckleballer, and Cy Perkins, a sturdy little catcher. Mr. Mack seemed to like me from the start—I could play any infield position with bounce, knew all the moves and had a strong arm. He tolerated my weak hitting. I pulled everything and had trouble hitting breaking pitches. During spring training in 1923 and 1924 he cured me of my pulling habit by assigning Eddie Collins as my coach. Eddie had been a member of the championship Athletics of the early 1910's; he was a scientific hitter with a .333 lifetime average. He charged me a Coke for every time I slapped a ball to left. It was a costly deal, for I'd pull now and then to break the monotony of going with the pitch through the middle or to right. But I learned and by '24 raised my average 50 points to .312 and from then on became a real major-leaguer with the bat.

Mr. Mack had an uncanny way of influencing his players which was contrary to the methods of those rough-and-ready times. He was the direct opposite of John J. McGraw, the much-publicized Little Napoleon of the New York Giants. Mr. Mack was not dictatorial like McGraw. He did not make the air blue with curses when something went wrong. He rarely used profanity, but when he did—look out! He spoke in a voice scarcely louder than parlor conversation, sitting on the bench in sober street clothes, looking like a deacon who'd wandered into the ball park by mistake. In his hand was the scorecard he'd wave to realign his defenses or to give signs. He controlled us and the ball game with very little effort but control us he did.

He was, without seeming so, a strict disciplinarian. He'd lay into miscreants with quiet sarcasm. If the offense was repeated, the offender would soon be handed a railroad ticket to some other destination, major or minor. We knew he was on the warpath when he came into the clubhouse walloping a wad of gum. He was chewing hard as he shut the clubhouse door one day in mid-July 1930. He called a meeting and opened it by declaring that he was going to call a spade a spade. We were the same outfit that had won the world's championship the previous October but now we were lagging in fourth place. Without raising his voice, he laced into every one of us. "It's up to you," he concluded. "You can win this pennant if you want to. If you don't keep on playing like the walking dead. That's all I have to say."

We won that day. We won the next. We romped through the rest of the season to another pennant and Series' triumph. We did it because we'd heard the truth about ourselves, spoken with convincing sincerity.

In Chicago's Comiskey Park a ball shot past me into left field. Al Simmons was rather slow in retrieving the ball and the runner scored from second on his throw. After the side was retired I glared at Al and kept glaring.

"Well, say it!" he snapped.

"If you're the left fielder, play like one!" I shot back. "You could of thrown that man out if you'd tried!"

One word led to another. The air was hot with blasts and counterblasts. From the end of the bench came Mr. Mack's voice. "Shut up, you two."

I continued to pop off. Mr. Mack came toward me. "Will you shut your g.d. mouth, Dykes," he quietly ordered.

I nearly fell off the bench. It was as close to profanity as I'd ever heard him go. I was so stunned that I lost my voice.

As a peacemaking gesture I joined Al as the inning ended and we went on field together. "We sure got the Old Man mad," said Al with a laugh.

"Did you hear that g.d.?" I chortled.

Another player told me later that, as we went on the field, Mr. Mack had chuckled. "Know what those two are saying? They're gloating over getting the Old Man mad."

Which didn't make me feel better—the Old Man had proved he could read our minds.

I knew Mr. Mack in the prime of maturity and the feebleness of great age, in glorious triumph and tragic adversity. When he was deep in his eighties he ended his 49-year management of the A's and put me in his place. He continued to follow the team's fortunes, motoring from city to city in a chauffeured car, sitting in a field box during games. I invited him to sit on the bench with us.

"No, Jimmie," he said. "You're the manager. The responsibility and the rewards are yours."

Connie Mack operated the Athletics with very little capital. He was an old ballplayer who regarded his team as a priceless trust. He guided it through the dark years of the early Twenties and into the bright championship years that followed, leaving an indelible mark on baseball. His memory is revered in the city of Philadelphia. To me he was the gentleman in professional sports.

The Athletics were in the midst of a seven-year slump. They had won four pennants in the five years between 1910 and 1914, then had dropped into the basement in '15 and were still resting there as late as 1921.

I boarded a train for Jacksonville in March 1918. A chronic tailender is easy to break into. The roster changed every day. We had three teams: one going, one playing, and one on its way to join us. I played beside has-beens, never-weres, and raw kids like myself, eager to make good.

Life in camp was rugged. Seven hours of daily running, fielding, and hitting; then, after a week, intersquad games. We reported at 9:30 A.M., walked the mile and a half from the hotel to the ball park, worked out until noon, when we tramped to the hotel for lunch. We hustled back to the ball park, worked out until 4:30, when we trudged back to the hotel to sink wearily onto our beds. It was a rough routine for fellows who did not keep themselves in the round-the-calendar physical condition of today's big-leaguers.

Clubhouse facilities at Jacksonville were primitive, lockers huddled together in an old wooden shed. The weather was hot and sticky, the water warm and rusty, air conditioning a dream of the far future. From mid-March until the season opened in April we barnstormed in small towns all over the South. Barnstorming was precisely what we did—we dressed in many a barnlike structure that would have sent cows and pigs gasping into the open air.

We trained in Montgomery, Alabama, from 1919 until 1924 when we invaded the wilds of Florida. And wilds they were: we traveled in private automobiles from Fort Myers to undeveloped Sarasota, riding rough roads that sometimes ended suddenly in what looked like jungle trails. I said to the driver, "How do you know which road to take?" "They all end in the same place, so what's the difference?" he replied.

As the years passed, buses with straight-backed seats carried us from town to town on barnstorming trips. For one three-day visit to Miami we used private automobiles over the Tamiami Trail. It was hard on the spine, but we took it as a matter of course.

On longer trips we rode the railroads, the rookies sleeping in upper berths, the regulars below. We saw the country close up, including some of the worst hotels built anywhere. It was all in the day's work.

The "Blue Shirt Express" was a feature of my Chicago White Sox spring training trips in the 1930's. We trained in Pasadena and scheduled a two-week jaunt cross country either with the Pittsburgh Pirates, who trained at Riverside, or the Chicago Cubs, who trained at Avalon on Catalina Island. Games were played every day in a different town. We'd leave after each game and had no chance to have our laundry done. So we'd wear blue shirts which didn't show the dirt—we called them "thousand milers." We'd start with four or five shirts and rush them to a laundress as soon as we arrived in Chicago.

We slept on the train, never saw the inside of a hotel. The same three Pullman porters clamored for ball-club assignments each spring. We had three Pullmans and a club car and we'd talk baseball from morning to midnight. The club car had no food; we ate in local "greasy elbows" on the way. Few of the parks where we played had adequate showers. The itinerary given us before we left California told us where we could find hot and cold running water for tub baths. The train was parked on a siding. We slept late, dressed and went into town for breakfast, then took a cab to the ball park. It was life al fresco and an important part of our education in baseball.

One day we went to a hotel in a small New Mexican town which was the worst I've ever seen. We hunted for a shower room and found there was none. We took turns in a zinc-lined bathtub, the only "rinsery" we could find. The water oozed out of the faucet drop by drop. We were late arriving at the ball park, still smelling of the sweat of yesterday's game, dreaming of the rivers, lakes and ocean we'd find when we reached civilization. We played that day to about twelve thousand people, no fences, no stands, just baseball in the open desert. The local team was operated by honest men—there were no turnstiles but we were paid every cent.

Travel during the season was de luxe. The Athletics' longest run was to St. Louis on a crack train. We left Philadelphia after dark and arrived in St. Louis the following evening. We played cards, read, talked baseball or slipped a pillow under our heads and snoozed. In our own private car we could smoke at will.

The coming of jet travel has ended the old fraternal jollity of the Pullmans, where informal baseball seminars were held, where batterymen discussed their strategy in coming games, where we beat the brains of baseball writers for gossip of the circuit, where we learned to know our teammates intimately and developed team spirit. Jet travel reminds me of the old Army bromide, "Hurry up and sit down!" I remember a jet trip from New York to Baltimore, a rush to Newark Airport, twenty-three minutes in the air, a rush into the city of Baltimore, registering at the hotel, and then sitting for twenty-four hours of an off-day. No matter how many times one flies, the fear of a missing motor, a fogbound port, a forced landing or a crash still lurks in the back of the mind. Jetting may be modern but give me the comfort and ease of a Pullman chair car, the chatter, the gags, the absence of worry, real or imaginary, the passage of idle time!

Give me those springs when I unkinked my muscles in Texas hamlets, took long, slow trips on wheezing trains through the Rio Grande Valley. I'm an old fud-dud, I guess!

Yes, give me those long dusty Texas springs when I ate dust on an unfenced field, snared grounders on rocky diamonds, shivered when a nor'easter blew, shook tarantulas out of my pants before putting 'em on, ate slop in dinky inns built when the golden West was being gilded. I was handed three dollars a day for meal money . . . that's all, mate, that's all.

But I loved it. I loved baseball. I was a big-leaguer. What more could a young fellow ask?

My stay with the Athletics in the spring of 1918 was brief. I found greetings from the President of the United States in my mailbox soon after the season opened. Off I went to Camp Greenleaf, Georgia, to make the world safe for democracy. I had weighed out of my baseball uniform at 159 pounds. In April 1919, when I received my discharge from the Army, I weighed in at 195. Mr. Mack ordered me to report to the team in New York. The following day I was playing third. Brick Owens was umpiring behind me. "You look like a barrel with a rope around the middle," he cracked. "That's to keep me from coming apart at the seams," I cracked back.

Mr. Mack used me at second base during most of the 59 games I played after my discharge. Despite my oversized fanny I darted around the infield, pivoted on double plays like a fancy Dan. I only batted .217 that year but I was convinced I'd cinched my job. I was sure of it when I was told to report to the Athletics' camp in the spring.

No sooner had the 1919 season begun than Mr. Mack took me aside, threw an arm about my shoulders. "Jimmie, my boy," he said, "I'm going to do something for you. I'm sending you to Atlanta to work yourself into real fine shape.

I gulped. "Thank you, Mr. Mack," I managed to say.

The diamond in Atlanta's Ponce de Leon Park was neatly manicured, the wooden stands freshly painted, but the clubhouse was a shack that would have gone up in smoke if a lighted match had been dropped on the floor. The weather was so hot that within days I'd sweated myself down to 178 pounds with no other exercise than ball-playing. I was the Crackers' second baseman, sandwiched between shortstop Chick Galloway and first-baseman Irv Griffin in a double-play combination that a local sportswriter dubbed "Through Death Valley" from the speed with which we two-timed runners. We didn't jell as a team until after the Fourth of July, when we were in last place. Suddenly we hit a pennant-winning pace, 30 victories in 32 games, as seasoned players returned from the armed forces. Among them was Bing Miller, who later became a longtime member of the Athletics, a lifetime .312 batter, and a close friend of mine.

I reported to the Athletics in the spring of 1920, full of vim, vigor and excess verbiage. On opening day I played second base. We lost. We lost 106 more times that season and wound up deep in last place. Some smart baseball writer called us the "White Elephants," a dead weight on the American League.

That was a historic year in baseball. The Black Sox scandal burst and the worried magnates named Judge Kenesaw Mountain Landis as High Commissioner to restore confidence in the game. They also noted that Babe Ruth was walloping home runs and decided to liven the dead ball and ban the spitter to stimulate hitting as a sort of box-office pep pill.

We Athletics didn't notice the difference. We seldom hit the ball for more than singles. "This judge ought to investigate what's keeping us in the league," I cracked. While learning how to take defeats without breaking down in tears I was earning the huge salary of $300 a month and supporting a loving wife. I played in every game despite bruises, mashed fingers, and lesser miseries. Laying off was dangerous. Bench-warmers were lying in wait, eager to take my job. Mr. Mack must have signed 500 players that season. I'd shake hands with a newcomer and show him around the clubhouse. I'd miss him a few days later. "What's happened to Joe Gadzooks?" I'd ask. "On his way to Oshkosh," I'd be told. Life was short at Shibe Park. I was already an old fixture, like the squeaky turnstile at the bleacher gate.

The Athletics' seven-year burial ended in 1922 when we pushed our noses above ground and into the rare air of seventh place. I was a whiz—I hit .274 and had the honor of leading the league in chances accepted at third base. In later years Bing Miller used to say that I fielded hot shots on my chest. It wasn't true then and I wouldn't swear it was true later, when I was kicking forty.

Things were happening in baseball, but not at Shibe Park. Babe Ruth was clouting more home runs than seemed possible. George Sisler was hitting over .400. Ty Cobb was still streaked lightning on the bags, and he was always on the bags. The New York Yankees were winning pennants. The whole country was excited about baseball except at Shibe Park.

It seemed unlikely that Mr. Mack would ever get the Athletics above the .500 mark. He had no money, unlike the millionaire colonels who owned the Yankees, and attendance was small at Shibe Park. He had no farm system, just a few scouts and many friends who tried to find razzle-dazzle rookies for him. He had no TV subsidy, because there was no TV then, not even radio. He had a few established players, hope and patience, and the ability to recognize a winning player when he saw one.

Just when he began to fashion the team that was to dominate the league a few years later, is difficult to say. We finished sixth in 1923, a small gain. Then, the following spring, Max Bishop joined us. Max was delivered by Mr. Mack's best baseball friend, Jack Dunn, owner of the Baltimore Orioles. Dunnie was a minor-league operator who kept his machine in high by developing talented youngsters and then selling them to the majors. Max reported at our camp in Montgomery, and immediately took possession of second base. He was a flashy fielder, smooth and sure. He also was as able a lead-off man as I've ever seen, not a dangerous hitter but a man who could work his way on and then go. His judgment of pitched balls was so keen that umpires automatically called a ball when Max took a pitch. Whether it came in inside or outside, high or low, they accepted his judgment as their own. At last we had a man who could get on base, a play-maker in the field, a deft handler of the bat, a run-maker, a live wire.

That spring also marked the debut of Al Simmons, a rangy outfielder who could hit for distance although he violated a basic rule in the batter's book. "That kid'll never make it," said a scout the day Al first worked out. Batting from the right side of the plate Al pulled back his left foot as the pitch came toward him, meanwhile leaving his right foot deep in the batter's box, a stance that quickly earned for him the nickname of "Bucketfoot Al." Yet, despite his unorthodox style, he was able to get power from his body into his swing. Triples, doubles, homers rattled off his bat. The Philadelphia newspapers called him a "phenom."

On opening day a photographer asked Al to pose with his foot in a red water bucket. He refused and came cussing into the clubhouse.

"What's wrong, kid?" I asked.

"Oh, some cheese picture-taker out there wants me to pose with one foot in a water bucket!"

"If I could hit like you I'd pose with one foot in a bucket of glue." After a long argument I induced Al to go on field and pose.

Mr. Mack took Al's odd style for granted. "Have you always hit like that?" he asked.

"It's the only way I know."

"Then keep on doing it, son."

Al kept bucketfooting for a 21-year lifetime average of .334 that won him a niche in baseball's Hall of Fame. In '24 his .308 hitting helped us gain the respectability of fifth place.

That fall Mr. Mack bought the entire Portland club of the Pacific Coast League and tossed in another $50,000 for Mickey Cochrane, a kid catcher hailed as a coming star. In camp the following spring Mickey was a ball of fire. He was exceptionally fast on his feet for a big fellow and, besides, a faultless receiver. But, to the surprise of those of us who'd been around long enough to know, he was weak on pop flies, fair or foul.

Mr. Mack assigned Kid Gleason, the fiery old Oriole, to hit pop-ups to Mike. Day after day the doughty Kid popped up until Mike learned how to discard his mask quickly, scan the skies for the ball and then clutch it as it came down. He became our No. 1 catcher from opening day and, because of his hitting and speed, our No. 3 batter, compiling a .331 average in his rookie year. I've never seen a quicker study than Mike, the perfect catcher, his manager's model manager in the field.

Among Mr. Mack's scouts was Franklin Baker, who'd earned the title of Home Run Baker on the championship team of the 1910's. Frank was scouring the Eastern Shore of Maryland for talent, driving on a country road, when he stopped to ask a plowboy for directions to the next town. The strapping young giant picked up his plow and pointed to the horizon. "It's thataway, sir."

Amazed by this show of strength, Frank asked: "By any chance do you play baseball?"

"Sure do," said Jimmy Foxx. "I'm on the town team."

From that day until he reported to us toward the end of the 1925 season, Jimmy was never far from the watchful eyes of the old home-run hitter. He had been a catcher, but Mr. Mack shifted him to first base and occasionally into my private territory around third base.

In the course of these experiments with our new-found power hitter I sat on the bench one day as Jimmy played my corner. A line drive bounced off Jimmy's shins for a hit. He muffed a ground ball. I turned to Mr. Mack. "So you think Foxx is a better third baseman than me, do you?"

He eyed me with a look that made me shiver. "No,

he isn't. But he can hit a darned sight farther than you can."

Jimmy overpowered the ball. He walloped some of the longest drives in history. In 1932 his 58 home runs ended Babe Ruth's string of six major-league titles. He batted over .300 in eleven of his first twelve seasons, his highest mark .356. He played every position in the lineup, pitching a win in 1945 when he was thirty-eight years old. Jimmy was a physical marvel as well as a man with the enthusiasm of a small boy.

Lefty Gomez, who couldn't have hit a tennis ball with paddle, still startles listeners by claiming that he holds the record for the longest home run of them all, more than 500 feet into the last box in Yankee Stadium's left-field third tier. After a pause to let his statement sink in, Lefty explains: "At least I started it on its way by throwing it to Jimmy Foxx."

We finished second in 1925. At last we had a contending team, a team on the make. That year Jack Dunn sent us a southpaw whose awesome speed was to thrill fans as much as Foxx's slugging feats. I first saw Lefty Grove pitch in Sunday exhibition games in Baltimore where we played to put dollars in the cashbox to replace those lost because of Pennsylvania's blue laws. He fanned some twelve to fourteen of us, for we had no intention of being skulled in an exhibition game and merely waved at his wild pitches.

Lefty was still wild in his rookie year in Philadelphia. He was a proud competitor, convinced that his was the greatest arm in baseball history. He worked hard to gain control; within two years he was putting the ball over the plate in a sizzling 20-game victory season.

Lefty was a holy terror on the mornings of his starts.

He'd report in a glower and keep glowering until the game began. He'd speak to none of us, spending a half hour on the rubbing table, eyes closed, until it was time to go on the field. He snarled at writers, ignored his teammates, seemed to hate humanity. In fact he was concentrating on the coming game, the batters he'd face, the goal he'd set for himself—winning every game he pitched.

Lefty led the American League in winning percentage five times and in earned-run averages eight. He was fiercely proud of his ability to blow batters down. He was leading Cleveland 5 to 1 in the seventh inning when Max Bishop muffed a grounder and on the next play I kicked the ball around. Runners were on first and second with none out instead of no one on and two gone. After I'd retrieved the ball I took it to Lefty in the box. He made a sour crack, I told him where to shove the ball. He began to lob pitches to the Indian batters. Two runs scored before he retired the side.

I grumbled out loud as I went to the bench. Mr. Mack heard my remarks. "So you want Grove out of there?" he asked.

"He don't want to pitch, does he?"

Mr. Mack called out to Eddie Collins: "Tell Quinn to get ready." Jack Quinn, our veteran spitballer, needed little time to get ready. He was in the box when the eighth began. He held the Indians scoreless the rest of the way.

On days when he wasn't starting Lefty would moan. "I'm not going to the bullpen today." Then our pitcher would wobble a little and Lefty would get up, pace the dugout, and suddenly leave for the bullpen. Finally Mr. Mack would decide to take the pitcher out. "Is Grove ready?" he'd ask Eddie Collins. Eddie would wave to the bullpen. In would come the great Grove. That's all we needed. Lefty would pour it on. We seldom lost when he was in the box.

In '31 Lefty won ten games in a row. Then Mr. Mack sent him in to relieve against the White Sox with the score tied, 1 to 1. His string of consecutive wins was broken in the top of the eleventh when Luke Appling and Lew Fonseca hit back-to-back home runs.

After the game Lefty dashed into the clubhouse, dove into street clothes and headed for the great out-of-doors. In the parking lot stood his new Pierce-Arrow, the prestige car of the day. He leaped into it and drove breakneck to his home in Lonaconing, Maryland, where he remained for five days. Then he returned to the fold, winning a game that was the first of sixteen straight victories.

Even Mr. Mack could find no way of punishing Lefty for going AWOL.

We were a bunch of gay, rollicking players who took delight in winning. I had fun in every game I played. All of us took defeats in stride—you can't win 'em all, can you?

But to Lefty victory was a matter of life and death. He suffered the agonies of the damned every time he lost a ball game. His morning sulks annoyed us, but we stood 'em for we knew that Lefty would always give his all to win.

I'm glad to say that he is a charming, white-haired gentleman today, the fires of youth quenched.

2

IT'S NICE UP THERE

ALL THAT STOOD in our way to a pennant were the Yankees. They not only beat us regularly in the days when we'd been the footstool of the American League, they rubbed our noses in the dirt. A long lead in early innings never satisfied the brutes of Murderers' Row. They kept pouring it on in late innings when five o'clock lightning would complete the job. We gave them some resistance in '26 when we finished third. We were second to their devastating '27 team and really began to feel our strength in '28.

I had a fixation about the Yanks. To put it exactly— I hated them. I always played my best against them.

They never stopped. They were remorseless, rabid. They drank our blood and thirsted for more. They kept right on hitting until they were weary and we were flat.

I undertook a personal vendetta against them. On October 2, 1925, I had my revenge. I went five for five in a game that we won, 10 to 0. I don't know how many runs I drove in that day. I got four of my five hits off Garland Braxton, a pretty good screwball artist, if I do say so myself. Herb Pennock mopped up that day. He kept shaking off his catcher, Benny Bengough, when I was at the plate. I didn't know why until I realized that I'd been hitting Braxton's first pitches and Pennock didn't want to put his own first pitch where I could get at it.

I don't know what Pennock threw me. I hit it safely for what probably is a record, five hits on just five pitches—and huzzah!—against the damn Yanks!

Mr. Mack didn't waste energy hating them. He went about the job of catching up to them with the calmness of an architect putting the finishing touches to the blueprints of a masterpiece. From Pittsburgh he obtained Mule Haas, an automated fly-catching machine, to play center field. Mule was Mike Drennan's baby. Drennan had scouted Mule in Atlanta, where the finishing touches were being put to him. On Mike's recommendation Mr. Mack bought the hard-hitting kid and was never sorry for it.

In 1926 Mr. Mack had traded Bing Miller to the St. Louis Browns. Bing was a rifle-armed right fielder and one of the greatest curve-ball hitters in the game. Despite his .331 and .325 averages during two seasons with the Browns, Mr. Mack succeeded in wangling him back to the Athletics in 1928. The outfield of Simmons,

Haas and Miller, who could go get 'em and also put 'em where they couldn't be gotten, was complete.

By then he had also plugged the gap at shortstop. Joe Boley was a veteran minor-leaguer whom Jack Dunn had kept on the Oriole payroll by giving him a salary equal to what he would have received in the majors, where he rightfully belonged. He succeeded Chick Galloway, my old Atlanta side-kick, and proceeded to seal off many an enemy rally with his fancy footwork, sure hands and strong arm. Teamed with Bishop he gave us the pitcher's best friend, a double-play-making shortstop at the pivot.

In that year of 1927, Mr. Mack surveyed our pitching and came up with important help. Grove was immense with 24 wins, but Lefty couldn't do it alone. Ed Rommel was still puzzling hitters with his knuckler, but Ed was not the man. Rube Walberg, who'd been with us since '23, had never quite measured up to his potential. (I did not know why until I managed the White Sox in '34. He was to start the game against us that day and I was telling my players what I knew about him at a clubhouse meeting. "We know how to beat this guy," said a player. "Watch him closely and he'll give away his pitches." Reading an opposing pitcher was a trick we Athletics had successfully used, but we'd never bothered to notice whether other teams were reading our boxmen. Now I learned that when Rube bent his wrist a curve was coming. The entire league had learned about this giveaway through the grapevine, which accounted for Rube's failure to star.)

Nevertheless Rube had a good year in '28 with 17 wins. He was our No. 3 starter behind Grove and Rommel.

We needed a fourth starter, preferably a right-hander, and from Baltimore came just the man that spring. George Earnshaw was a big, strong, fast-ball pitcher with a sharp-breaking curve. He threw his leg in the batter's face as he reared back to deliver the ball. Unlike Grove, George was a gay blade who took life as it came his way. He had no nerves, a tireless arm, and could pitch with two days' rest, if necessary. He was used sparingly during his rookie year, but by '29 he was what we needed most, a right-handed stopper.

In '28 seven of us hit over .300. I was the slacker at .277. We won 98 games, enough to capture most pennants. But the damn Yankees won 101 and we were still second best.

I was the handyman during these years. I played all infield positions, including first base, filled in in the outfield—and pitched. Dolly Gray was leading the Boston Red Sox in the seventh inning one day in 1927 when he filled the bases. Some of my friends behind third base set up a howl for me to take the pitcher's box. Mr. Mack yielded to their pleas and in the eighth I took Dolly's place on the mound. I showed a fast ball and a bit of a knuckler I'd developed on the sidelines. I held the Red Sox to two hits and no runs the rest of the way.

One of the reasons for my wandering was that Mr. Mack had obtained Sammy Hale, a good-hitting third baseman from Detroit 'way back in '21, and alternated us at that position. Sammy hurt his back late in '28. His career ended the following year, enabling me to settle down as a full-time third sacker.

I was typical of the major-leaguers of the Twenties. I seriously studied the form of friends and foes but I had my fun, too. I was third in the trio of needlers, Bing Miller, Mule Haas and myself, thinking up cute tricks to rattle the opposition, arguing with umpires, chattering to fans. We were full of the old-time Harry. We were young, we were on a rising team, we had comrades we admired and a manager we respected. What more could we want?

1929 was the year of the Great Crash. By the end of September the only stock that wasn't tumbling was that of the Philadelphia Athletics. We were walking away with the flag. Everything was clicking, including me. I was batting well over .300. I no longer had a morbid fear of the curve ball. I could hit anything, anywhere. I met the ball where it was pitched, which is the sure key to .300 hitting.

I was always in top physical shape. I drank nothing harder than beer. My only vice was smoking, or chewing on a good cigar when I wasn't smoking. I played golf and bowled during the off-season. I lived at home with a loving wife who had brought three fine children into the world. I was making the fabulous salary of $10,000 a year and having fun making it.

Thanks to Mr. Mack's light hand we played with light hearts. His scorecard was a magic wand. His head was full of accurate information about every player in the league. When he waved the card we moved into the positions he designated, even Ty Cobb, who had ended his sensational career with us in 1928. Ty had always played as he pleased. During a game with the Washington Senators Mr. Mack signaled for Ty to move about fifteen feet back for Goose Goslin. Ty ignored the magic card until we infielders shouted: "Go back! Go back!" Ty finally obeyed.

Goslin's hot drive landed in Ty's glove exactly where

Mr. Mack had ordered him to go. It was the final out of the inning. Ty ran grinning to the bench. "That's the first time anyone's told me where to stand," I heard him say. "Mr. Mack, you had it exactly right!"

The 1929 Athletics had thunderous hitting, masterful pitching, and a dazzling defense. Every man in the lineup hit over .300 except our defensive stars, Bishop and Boley. The Yankees had been stricken by the death of Manager Miller Huggins.

We won the flag by 19 games.

I was about to experience the once-in-a-lifetime thrill of my first World Series. The big games were to start in Chicago where we'd meet the Cubs of canny Joe Mc-Carthy, who'd made a runaway race in the National League, too.

We rode into Chicago brimming with confidence. Betting odds favored us; fans across the nation were impressed by our strength. We were certain that Grove, Earnshaw and Walberg would outpitch their starters, Charlie Root, Pat Malone and Guy Bush, and hold their best hitters, Riggs Stephenson, Kiki Cuyler, Hack Wilson and Rogers Hornsby.

I was as cocky as ever as I took batting practice. I did my stuff in fielding practice, then flopped onto the bench beside Al Simmons.

"Hey, Jim, look who's warming up!" exclaimed Al. "Wonder what's happened to Grove?"

I looked. Howard Ehmke was tossing 'em on the practice mound. "Yes, something must be wrong with Grove."

Down the bench was Mr. Mack. "What's the matter with you two?"

"If Ehmke's good enough for you he's good enough for us," rejoined Al.

Howard Ehmke was the thirty-three-year-old "spot" pitcher who hadn't started for seven weeks because he'd been out scouting the Cubs for us. He'd won seven games as the No. 5 man on our seven-man staff. What on earth had got into Mr. Mack's head?

We soon found the answer to that puzzler. Ehmke pitched from a sidearm delivery with an assortment of curves and an offspeed fast ball that set the equally right-handed Cub hitters back on their heels. Foxx broke the scoreless tie in the seventh inning with a jolting drive into the left center-field bleachers for a home run. Charlie Root went out for a pinch hitter in the Cubs' half. We picked up two unearned runs in our ninth.

Meanwhile, Ehmke had been immense, fanning twelve. One was out in the Cubs' last turn at bat when Kiki Cuyler sent a sharp ground ball my way. I fielded it cleanly, but threw low and under Foxx's glove for a two-base error. Stephenson promptly brought Cuyler home with a single.

My chin was down to my ankles. My spirits revived as old Howard made a pinch hitter roll into a force play. Then Charlie Tolson, a second pinch hitter, took a third strike on a floater. It was the thirteenth strikeout, a Series record.

"Credit that thirteenth strikeout to me," I chirped as the clubhouse celebration got under way. "Tolson never would have been to bat if I hadn't put Cuyler on."

And credit Mr. Mack for the masterly strategy of starting Ehmke instead of Grove. He'd gambled that the crafty right-hander could stop the powerful right-hand Cub hitters. It was the surprise hat trick, pulling a rabbit out of a topper, and it won.

We were one up on the Cubs . . .

Ehmke had begun his big-league career with Detroit while Ty Cobb was managing. He had good stuff but a mediocre record. "You'll never amount to beans unless you dust off the good hitters," warned Ty. "Go out there and knock 'em down!"

The mild-mannered kid failed to heed this advice and was traded to the Red Sox. In his first start against the Tigers he faced Ty Cobb. His first pitch to Ty went directly to his ex-manager's head. Off came Ty's cap as he hit the dust. Bat in hand he advanced on Howard, spitting choice threats. "What are you so mad about?" Ehmke shouted. "Didn't you tell me to knock down the good hitters? And aren't you the best of 'em all?"

Ty stopped in his tracks. "So I did . . . so I did," he muttered. He retreated and, believe it or not, struck out.

Mr. Mack sent right-handed George Earnshaw against the Cub righties in the second game. Our big bats rapped out six runs in the fifth inning, but the Cubs touched up George for three tallies in the sixth. Grove came out of the bullpen to put down the uprising. We won, 9 to 3.

After a day's interval for travel Earnshaw was back in the box as the third game began in Philadelphia. This time George went nine innings but wound up on the losing end of a 3 to 1 score as Guy Bush silenced our bats.

Undeterred, Mr. Mack continued with his right-hand starters the next day. Old Jack Quinn was his choice. At forty-five, Jack was one of the few surviving spitballers, a relic of the dead-ball days used mainly in relief during the season. "We better play deeper than usual," I told Boley before the game.

Jack held the Cubs for three innings, but they got to him for two runs in the fourth and knocked him out with five runs in the fifth and made it 8 to 0 with one more off Ed Rommel in the sixth. Meanwhile, Charlie Root had been mowing us down.

All was quiet on our bench. "Take your last licks," said Mr. Mack. "I'm sending in substitutes for you the next inning."

Simmons opened our seventh with a mighty blast over the left-field roof. At least we won't be shut out, I thought. No one got excited when Foxx and Miller singled. I shut my eyes and got a one-baser that sent Foxx home, making it 8 to 2. "I think Root's losing his stuff," said Mr. Mack. To Boley he said, "Swing at anything that comes near the plate, Joe." Joe swung and his single brought Miller in with run No. 3.

George Burns pinch-hit for Rommel and popped out, but Bishop smacked another single and I trotted over the plate. Root was out. We'd cut the Cubs' long lead in half. Joe McCarthy called in Artie Nehf, the veteran southpaw.

Mule Haas was up. He met a fast ball solidly and whacked it high into center field. Hack Wilson started in for it, hesitated, backtracked, apparently blinded by the sun. I leaped up. The ball was heading for deepest center field. Now everyone in the dugout was up. I stood at the railing as the ball struck the center-field wall. Boley and Bishop were in. Haas was heading for third . . . rounding third. "He's gonna make it!" I cried. "There he goes!" On went Mule, sliding. "We're in the ball game!" I clouted a player on the back. "Hurray!"

Only I hadn't clouted a player. I'd knocked Mr. Mack off his feet and into the bat rack. I grabbed him about the waist and hauled him to his feet. I must have had a funny look on my face, for he reached out and patted me on the arm. "That's all right, Jimmie. Anything goes at a time like this. Isn't this wonderful?"

I'd knocked down a manager and gotten away with it!

I didn't know the score. I was too excited to look at the scoreboard. Nehf was walking Cochrane and walking himself out of the game. Sheriff Blake came in to pitch for the Cubs. I couldn't hear myself think, the pandemonium was so great. Simmons singled. Foxx singled.

Now burly Pat Malone was in the box. Malone plunked Miller in the ribs. The bases were full and I was up for the second time in the inning. I had just one idea in mind. I had to hit the ball, rip it, knock its cover off . . .

Malone set me up with a strike across the letters. I knew what was coming. Malone was a fast-ball pitcher. Another fast one was coming. I got set. I swung. The crack of my bat was sweet music for my ears. As I rounded first I saw Stephenson chasing the ball. I headed for second, slid, made it. Simmons and Foxx were home!

I called time to take a peek at the scoreboard. I'd knocked in the ninth and tenth runs of the inning. We had scored ten runs in one turn at bat! It had to be a Series record!

Malone fanned Boley and Burns for the second and third outs.

We were pros, trained never to show our feelings, but we blew our stacks completely as we saw Lefty Grove warming up on the mound. We were on cloud nine as Lefty blew down six Cubs in the last two innings, fanning four of them.

One more win and we'd be champions of the world! Let's go, boys . . .

Mr. Mack returned to Ehmke for the fifth game. Howard didn't have it. He gave two runs in the third inning, then yielded to Rube Walberg. Pat Malone blanked us on two hits for eight innings. As our ninth began everyone was planning a quick dash to the train that would take us back to Chicago.

Bishop gave us a life by slapping a single to right.

Haas was up. He worked the count to 3 and 2. Malone came in with a fast ball. Mule swung from his toes. The ball carried high, hit the scoreboard, dented it.

The score was tied, 2 to 2!

Malone dug in. He reared back. He retired Cochrane on a hopper to second base. But he didn't have it for Simmons. Al raked one to right for a two-base hit.

Bing Miller was at the plate. Malone fed him fast balls to the count of 2 and 2. I was kneeling in the batter's circle. I sensed that Malone would try to cross up Bing with a curve. I jumped up. "Swing at the next one, Bing . . . swing!" I yelled.

And Bing, the classic curve-ball hitter, swung at the curve. The ball shot over the infield, rolled to the foot of the scoreboard. Simmons was zooming home with the winning run. He scored ——

We were champions, champions of the world! The Athletics were the greatest gang of ballplayers in the world, bar none, better than those damn Yankees had ever been. And I was one of them . . .

As Simmons scored, the crowd went berserk. Mayor Mackey of Philadelphia leaped from the field box where he'd been hosting President Hoover and hugged everyone in sight. When he returned, a Presidential aide remarked that no one leaves the presence of the Chief Executive of the United States without his permission.

"Don't be silly, man," grinned His Honor. "A Philadelphian does as he pleases on a day like this."

I was in the midst of a wild jamboree in the clubhouse. I'd batted .421 in the Series and knew it. I saw Judge Landis fighting his way from locker to locker. He threw his arms over Mickey Cochrane's shoulders. "When are you going to serve that cake and tea, Mike?" he needled.

It was the final jab in the battle of bench-jockeying between the Cubs and Athletics, a row featured by some pretty raw profanity. Cochrane had been the ringleader in the exchange of sultry language. The Cubs' nerves had been frayed by their defeats. Third base was not far from the Chicago dugout. My ears had burned every time I'd picked up my glove.

Landis had been seated between the dugouts and had heard the salty barrage. Fearing that ladies might be offended he had summoned the two managers to a meeting where he'd warned that he would hold them responsible for their players' blow-offs.

When Mr. Mack had passed on this warning, Mickey had exclaimed: "When do we serve cakes and tea? Between innings, like at cricket?"

The remark had gotten back to the Commissioner, who'd turned it back on Mike for a last laugh.

Landis himself was an artist in the use of profanity, interspersing his private conversation with words never found in unabridged dictionaries in those days. He even dropped four-letter words into his public lectures to offenders in such a way that they never seemed offensive. He was a man's man if there ever was one. But he was death on profanity that might be heard by women fans.

I was profane but never vulgar, merely emphatic, especially to umpires. Umpires usually ignored the profanity universally used by ballplayers in those days, but you'd get the thumb if you cast aspersions on their ancestry or hinted that their eyesight was something less than 20/20. Bill Guthrie, tall, massive above the waist, with a bull-like neck and jaw thrust forward, once told me: "When a player kicks or puts on a little demonstration, I got to listen to him. But when he calls me an s.o.b. or blind as a bat I know he wants the afternoon off and I give it to him."

Today's umpires are different. They don't give a player a chance to exercise his vocal cords. Soon they'll be carrying flasks of mouthwash in the pocket where they keep their whiskbrooms.

We bulled our way to the top of the American League in 1930. We romped to the finish, eight games ahead of Walter Johnson's Washington Senators. The St. Louis Cardinals, champions of the National League, were Johnnies-come-lately, a rowdy team with many colorful players, not the least of whom was Burleigh Grimes, their spitballing ace. Grimes needled us by calling us "those American League bushers" in print. He'd been a ball of fire in his own league, thanks to his remarkable control of the wet pitch.

He was on the mound in the Series opener, holding us to five hits to the Cardinals' nine off Lefty Grove. But two of ours were home runs by Simmons and Cochrane. Mickey got back at Grimes for the "busher" line by taunting him unmercifully as he rounded the bases. We won, 5 to 2, and were off and running.

Mike did it again the next day, homering off Flint Rhem as Earnshaw had one of his best days, winning 6 to 1. We rode the rails to St. Louis that night, cool and confident. It looked like a breeze.

The breeze whipped into a whirlwind. Wild Bill Hallahan blanked us, 5 to 0.

The fourth game brought Jess Haines in against Grove. It was in this tight battle that the goat's horns were pinned to my head. With the score tied, 1 to 1, in the fourth inning, Chick Hafey was on second. Ray Blades chopped the ball in my direction. From the corner of my eye I saw Hafey racing to third. I was not far from the bag and could have backtracked to tag him out. Instead I threw hurriedly to first, pulling Foxx off base. The ball rolled past him. Hafey scored and Blades was safe on my error. He tallied later on back-to-back singles.

My error was one of commission and stupidity. I called myself a rockhead for not beating Hafey to third. The two runs were decisive, for Haines held us to four hits and we lost, 3 to 1. The Philadelphia morning papers called me a numbskull. I was the home-town hero who'd let the home team down. Mr. Mack must have noticed my woebegone expression. He used the right psychology to wipe it off my face. "You went for the right play, Jimmy," he said. I wasn't so sure; words couldn't change the score. The Cards had pulled even with us.

Fortunately Earnshaw had his best stuff in the fifth game, holding the Cards to three hits. It was a scoreless tie for eight innings between big George and Grimes. Then Mr. Mack changed his strategy and ordered Mule Haas to bunt. Haas laid down a beauty and beat the throw to first, then stole second base. Boley also bunted. Grimes fielded the ball and tried to catch Haas at third. Mule slid in under the throw and Joe was credited with a hit. Then Mr. Mack sent Jim Moore in as a pinch hitter for Earnshaw, and Jim walked, filling the bases. But Bishop forced Haas at the plate and it was up to me.

I smacked a spitter hard, but straight at shortstop Charlie Gelbert, who threw me out. It was a big opportunity wasted. You can't win 'em all.

Grove was serving his fast ball in the Cards' eighth and retiring the Cards in order. Cochrane opened our ninth with a walk, but Grimes got Simmons on a pop-up. Now it was Foxx.

I don't remember what the count was as Foxx teed off. The ball vanished into the hands of some fan in the left center-field bleachers. The big St. Louis crowd sat stunned as Jimmy jogged around bags behind Cochrane.

That was all, man. We won, 2 to 0, and were within one game of another world's championship.

Two days later we were back in old Shibe Park, Earnshaw facing Hallahan. We were high and handsome. Wild Bill didn't have it, big George did. It was his third start in the Series. He shut out the Cards until the ninth when they got one run. Meantime, we'd cinched the game on seven hits, each good for one run. I clipped one over the fence, wiping out memories of my bonehead play in the fourth game. It felt good, that blow.

We were the champs again, invincible!

1931 was everyone's year. We rolled up 107 wins, finishing 13½ games ahead of the Yankees. Earnshaw won 21, Grove 31, including those strings of 10 and 16. He had lost only three games by the season's final day. Before the game with the Red Sox Mr. Mack announced that he would use three pitchers for three innings each in a tune-up for the Series. Lefty took over with the score tied, 1 to 1. In the ninth the Bostonians squeezed a run across.

Lefty bolted from the box, took to the clubhouse, showered and dressed without speaking to a soul. Then he vanished without a trace.

We were due to entrain for St. Louis at 7 that evening and assembled at the North Philadelphia station at 5:30. Lefty was not among us.

Minutes passed. Had he taken off again for his Maryland home? By 6:50 bets were being laid pro and con his appearance; heads were hanging from the train windows; reporters were peering down the stairs, each hoping for a first glimpse of the missing man.

At 6:59 I heard the cry, "Here he comes!" Lefty hove into view, strode to a car, hopped on.

I sighed with relief. Lefty would pitch the opening game.

He was in complete control of the Cardinals, outpitching young Paul Derringer, 6 to 2. Again we were on our way.

But Bill Hallahan held us to three hits the next day and we lost, 2 to 0, behind Earnshaw. We had a job on our hands, for this was not the same team we'd

beaten a year earlier. The difference was rookie Pepper
Martin in center field. He'd made three hits off Grove
and stolen a base. He didn't look like a star. He had
good speed but he was no Ty Cobb. But he hit the ball
and smashed his way around the bases on sheer nerve
and determination. In the second inning of the second
game he doubled, then took off for third. He slid in on
his belly, bowling into me, ripping open his uniform
shirt to expose a mat of thick hair on his booming chest.
He scored on a sacrifice fly. In the seventh he singled,
immediately he stole second, moving to third on a
ground ball and squirming home on a squeeze bunt.
He was no Man o' War in human form; he was more
like a catapult, hurling himself around the bases.

We almost caught up with Hallahan in our ninth. He
really got wild, walking Foxx and me. He fanned Dib
Williams for the second out, then faced Jim Moore,
who was pinch-hitting for Earnshaw. Moore took a
third strike which broke low, hitting the dirt. Jim
Wilson nonchalanted the ball to third-baseman Jake
Flowers.

Eddie Collins, our third-base coach, waved franti-
cally to Moore. Moore got the message and ran to first.
The game wasn't over, we had the bases full. Fans were
leaping on the field; the Cardinals surrounded the plate
umpire, howling for justice.

The umpire stood fast, as always. Wilson had
dropped the low curve, then thrown the ball to third.
Moore was safe on first.

And I was rooted to second, praying for Bishop to
single Foxx and me home with the tying runs.

Max couldn't do it. He popped a soft foul to first-
baseman Jim Bottomley.

The chatter in our clubhouse was all about Pepper

Martin. How could we stop him? "What's he been hitting?" Mr. Mack asked Earnshaw.

"Everything I've thrown up to him," said big George.

Back home in Philadelphia it was Grove and Grimes again. Grove was off form, possibly tired after his long season and his terrific efforts on opening day. He yielded twelve hits, two to the irrepressible Martin. Grimes was magnificent. He gave no hits in the first seven innings, a single in the eighth, and a home run by Al Simmons in the ninth with Cochrane on as the result of a walk. Al's blast over the right-field wall put us on the scoreboard but meant nothing else. Grove was tagged for twelve hits in a 5 to 2 rout.

Earnshaw made us forget Grove's lapse the next day, matching Grimes's two-hitter with one of his own. It was a 3 to 0 beauty but we failed to stop Martin. He stole another base.

And it was all Martin in the fifth game, a home run, two singles and a sacrifice fly off Waite Hoyt, the old Yankee schoolboy Mr. Mack had obtained in a trade. Hallahan did us in with a 5 to 1 shellacking. We trailed in the Series, two wins to the Cards' three.

"This is the game we've got to win," said Mr. Mack as we arrived in St. Louis for the sixth game. Grove got the message and so did our hitters. They banged in eight runs in two big innings for an 8 to 1 win. "Now George will finish it tomorrow," promised Mr. Mack.

St. Louis fans believed the same thing. There were many empty seats in Sportsman's Park for the grand finale, although it was a Saturday afternoon in fine October weather. Earnshaw had his usual stuff but gremlins gave the Cards a two-run lead in the very first inning. Two scratch hits—one on a looper that Dib Williams seemed to lose in the sun, another that fell between Simmons and me—started them off. A sacrifice, a wild pitch scored one run, the second came in on a dropped third strike. And the Cards made it 4 to 0 in the third on a single and a homer. This clout by George Watkins was the only solid blow off George, who retired the next eighteen hitters in a row.

When I think of that game I remember Grimes moistening the ball, then flinging it as we tried to connect with it and failed. I remember him standing in the middle of the diamond defying us and that feeling of frustration that came over us as inning after inning went by and we realized that we were going to lose. In the ninth Simmons wangled a walk and with two out I got four straight balls. Then young Williams, playing short in place of Boley, dropped a Texas leaguer into left and the bases were full. Up came Roger Cramer, batting for Walberg, who'd suceeded George in the box, and poked a single to center, scoring Miller, who'd got on by a force play, and me.

Two on, two out . . . Grimes was about through. Card Manager Gabby Street went to the mound and told him so. In came Bill Hallahan, who'd beaten us twice. Max Bishop was up—could he bring in the tying runs? Would we come from behind as we'd already done so many times?

Max took a ball, a strike, a ball, a third ball, a second strike. A fast ball was coming . . . Max swung. It was a solid blow, the ball rose over second and into center field. A Cardinal was racing toward it, Pepper Martin of course. Full tilt, glove outstretched, Martin caught it and did a little jig of triumph.

Well, it's been nice up there, boys, I thought.

It would never be quite as nice again.

THOSE GLORIOUS TWENTIES

MUCH MORE than a World Series ended with Martin's catch. The Athletics' domination of the baseball world came to an end. Never again would an independent owner like Connie Mack be able to put together a great ball club without financial support and a nationwide organization.

And, in a certain sense, the Twenties also ended that day, although the calendar said that it was 1931. We were a team of the Twenties, put together in that decade when the sky was still the limit for any American with ambition and go.

I'm no controversial character, but I'm getting into

one controversy with both feet and a loud voice. I'm one of those old-timers who believe that baseball reached its heights in the Twenties and has never been as good since then. We outhit the moderns by a big margin, we outran them, outpitched them, outplayed them. We played with dash, with spirit, with high morale, and, although we played for pay, mere money was not our major consideration. We played for sport, for the sake of the game, for the thrill of it. Call us naïve. Maybe we were. But we had fun playing.

By modern standards our pay was miserably low. In 1929 I earned $7,000 plus $5,231 as my Series share. In '31 I received $10,000 plus $3,023 as the loser's slice. I lost my Series check when the bank shut its doors one day after I had deposited it. In '32 Mr. Mack raised my salary to $13,000. I don't know what Grove or Foxx got, but it wasn't much more.

Mr. Mack was not the hardfisted employer that some have called him. He depended on current income to meet expenses. The Athletics played to slim crowds until '29. His payroll was roughly equal to that of other clubs except the Yankees.

Each winter I'd drop down to Shibe Park to talk salary with him, usually just before leaving for camp. In '28 I walked into John Shibe's office and found Mickey Cochrane there for the same purpose. Mr. Mack was in his office in the tower and word came down that he was ready to see Mike.

"Good luck, Grump," I called. I always called Mike "Grump" because when I roomed with him on the road he was grumpy mornings until he ate breakfast. I sat watching Shibe play solitaire until Cochrane came down.

"How'd you make out?" I asked.

"Connie's going to borrow off the next man he sees," he said.

Just then Mr. Mack walked in. He smiled as he put an arm about my shoulders. "Would you like to come up and talk to me, Jimmie?"

"No thanks, Mr. Mack," I said. "I can see you're in a very good humor this afternoon. So am I, so don't let's spoil it. I'll come back tomorrow if it's all the same to you."

I went back the next day and got all I asked for.

Baseball was baseball, pure and simple, in those days. We had no distractions, no added attractions, no stunts, no special days, nothing to divert us from our main job, which was to play as well as we could. Baseball was a living, a profession, the greatest game invented by man, and it was also our hobby. We old-timers enjoyed every minute of every game. We ribbed each other, needled the opposition, swapped gibes with the umpires, exchanged greetings with the fans. "Where've you been?" we'd ask a regular who hadn't shown up for a few days. When we became a settled team during our championship years we were all pals, a harmonious bunch of team players who helped each other on the field and off. We had no cliques, no factions, no holdouts, no nonsense.

My tongue was as busy at thirty-five as when I broke in at Gettysburg, fresh and twenty-one. I got in my digs, my wisecracks, my chatter every day. I had played against the best, against Ty Cobb, Tris Speaker, George Sisler, Rogers Hornsby, Frankie Frisch—and Babe Ruth. I may have hated the Yankees, but the Babe was something else again, a big happy guy who could loft skyscraping flies into distant pastures and go tripping around the bases on his undersized feet, a grin on his broad face. One day he hit one so high that it vanished into the deep blue sky as I tried to find it. My eyes watered from staring into the blue and it fell ten feet behind me. By then the Babe was loping into third base.

"That's the shortest triple I ever saw," I called out to Babe.

"Thanks to you, bud," he laughed.

On another occasion we were snarled with the Yanks in a long-drawn-out extra-inning game at Yankee Stadium. We went into an infield shift as the Babe came up in the fifteenth. Boley played third and I was at shortstop that day. I moved to the right of second and Joe moved into my position. There were runners on first and second.

Jack Quinn delivered one of his patented spitters. The Babe neatly dumped it along the third-base line. By the time Boley picked up the ball the runner on second was sprinting past and sliding safely home with the winning run. Babe had won the game with a measly bunt.

When I broke in, Ty Cobb was respected for his hitting and feared for his slashing base-running. I was feeling my oats in '22 when he came to town with his Tigers and I decided to stop his tearing around the sacks. I was playing second when he came flying into my base, spikes high. I called time and told Ed Rommel, who had a good pick-off motion, to throw to me on a count of five.

Ty took a long lead. On the five-count Rommel whirled and threw to me. I interposed my knee between Ty and the bag. "Out!" cried the umpire. It was the sweetest word I ever heard. Ty's face was purple.

"Wanta go to the hospital?" he snarled. "You cut me and you'll go too!" I snarled back.

He meekly retired from the scene.

Like many other players of those days Ty had a pet superstition. Whenever he came in from left field he would go out of his way to step on second base. I noticed this habit and decided to break it. For three innings I ran from the bench and stood on the bag, blocking him off. After the fourth inning he came glaring at me and gave me the hip. I hipped him back. His fists were clenched and I thought we might come to blows. Suddenly he laughed. "I guess I don't need any help to beat this lousy club of yours," he said. "I'll get my hits today just the same."

That day he got three of the 4,191 hits he made in his lifetime. He could say it with his bat, superstition or not.

Ty must have liked my standing up to him. Mr. Mack told me that in 1925 he had tried to buy me for his Tigers for the enormous sum of $50,000 but Mr. Mack had refused to sell me. It was a great compliment to me from a great star.

In '27 when Ty was forty-one, he was sold to the Athletics and batted .357; in '28, his final year, he hit a solid .327. One day in Cleveland he failed to hit safely the first two times up. The third time he was at the bat rack when Mr. Mack ordered a pinch hitter to take his place.

Ty's pained expression led Mr. Mack to explain: "I'm sending in a right-hand hittter to face this southpaw."

"Let me do the hitting!" Ty snapped. "I can hit any ball that's near the plate."

Mr. Mack called the pinch hitter back. "Go ahead and prove it, Ty," he said.

Ty grabbed his bat. He strode up to the plate and ripped a double to left on the first pitch.

There are no Ty Cobbs today, no Babe Ruths, no 30-game pitchers like Lefty Grove, no faultless control artists like Grover Cleveland Alexander, no wizards of the spitball like Burleigh Grimes. Grimes was one of the few licensed spitballers permitted to use saliva after the ban was ordered in 1920. Among others were Stan Coveleski, Urban Shocker, Al Sothoron, Red Faber, and our own Jack Quinn, dean of them all.

The spitter was a tough pitch to hit. It came up to the plate without a spin, then sharply broke down. Mixed with a fast ball and a curve it kept batters on their toes.

It was impossible to know when a spitter was coming. The pitcher usually chewed slippery elm to get his juice. He faked the spitter by holding his glove before his face with every delivery, working his jaws as if applying the juice. Red Faber was especially clever in faking; when he was preparing a spitter he never moved his jaws. Grimes was the toughest to hit; he controlled his spitter as accurately as his fast ball.

I think the ban on the spitter should be removed. It isn't "unsanitary," as nice Nellies used to charge. "Spit" is not a nasty word; or, if it is, let's call it the "saliva pitch" or the "moist ball." The spitter was outlawed because club owners wanted more hitting to divert the attention of the fans from the Black Sox scandal. The magnates also put jackrabbit into the ball for the same purpose.

I'm glad I didn't have to face more than a few spitball flingers. The licensed few knew every trick in the pitcher's book. They pitched many complete games, their careers were lengthened. They seldom suffered from sore arms.

Something resembling the spitter is thrown today. After his retirement Preacher Roe, the Dodger star of some fifteen years ago, confessed that he'd used it throughout his career. Hugh Casey's missed third strike in the '41 World Series was a spitter. Today at least one big-league pitcher in every five uses it, reliefers especially. It is their "out pitch" with men on bases or when the count goes to 3 and 2. They wet their fingers with spit or sweat from their brow, in the midst of a series of jerky motions that make them look like the victims of Saint Vitus's dance, tugging their caps, touching their letters, pulling up their belts, annoying the batter, the umpire and the fans.

The game is delayed when a batter, suspecting the pitcher of moistening the ball, asks the umpire to inspect it. The umpire seldom looks at it closely. He has seen a pitch break extra sharply. By the time he gets the ball in his hand it's been tossed from the catcher back to the pitcher and is as dry as the sand in the Mojave Desert. The umpire glances at it, tosses it back to the pitcher. Not one umpire in the majors today has ever seen a spitball pitcher in action. Rather than penalize a pitcher for a rule infraction that he cannot prove, he lets the guy get away with it.

Such folderol sickens me. When I was coaching the Kansas City Athletics I stopped a game and told the umpire that the opposing pitcher was throwing a spitter. "Jim," was the reply, "I've never seen a spitter yet and I'm not going to look for one now."

I failed to tell him that a member of our staff was throwing a "pomade ball" which he'd added to his repertory by slicking his fingers on the greasy stuff he applied to his hair before suiting up for the game.

A delivery which is perfectly legal but seldom used today is the overhand curve or "drop," as we used to call it when I was a boy. It breaks abruptly down, like an apple falling off a table. The overhand curve is a highly effective pitch and much easier on the arm than the popular slider, which is thrown like the genuine curve but breaks away instead of down. We used to call the slider the "sailer," because it sometimes takes off erratically, or "sails."

The slider harms the muscles of the upper arm and shoulder and jerks the elbow joint. When it fails to break it is easy to hit. "What did you throw him?" I've asked pitchers after the batter clouted a home run. "A slider that hung," they'd reply.

The overhand curve, coming down out of the shoulder, is hard to follow and must be met solidly to go safe. Tommy Bridges, the Tiger star of the 1930's, won nearly 200 games with his overhand curve. Johnny Murphy stopped many a Yankee opponent with it in his brilliant relief appearances. Jughandle Johnny Morrison of the Pirates broke his overhand curve down like the handle of a jug and was a 25-game winner in 1923. Camilo Pascual is the best of the current overhanders; he has fanned more than 200 batters a year four times with his now-you-see-it, now-you-don't delivery.

The Twenties were the period when the game reached a perfect synthesis of the far-flung home run and the delicate bunt, of brute power combined with subtle inside baseball. Big men perfected the art of driving the ball into the seats or out of the park;

smaller men used their wits to spray hits to all fields or bunted to upset defenses, to squeeze runs in, to give the fans the thrill of the unexpected. It was a live game then, never cut-and-dried as today. It was played in an amateur spirit by professionals who were amateurs at heart. It was a fun game, colorful, melodramatic. It was a Babe Ruth game, a game in which the Babe could pitch, play first, the outfield, run, throw, and hit homers, triples, doubles, singles, and also win games with perfectly placed bunts. It was everyone's game, played everywhere, and everyone could afford the price of a seat.

I was there. I know.

4

GO WEST, OLD MAN!

In 1932 the same eight regulars and the same three starting pitchers who had won three pennants and two world's championships were still around. The Athletics were still a relatively young team; I was the oldest at thirty-five, but I played in 153 games that year and drove in 90 runs on a .265 average. Foxx still banged out hits at a .356 rate, Simmons at .331. Grove was as blindingly fast as ever and a 25-game winner, Earnshaw won 25 and Walberg 17. We kept pace with the Yankees until late July, then slowly drifted 13 games behind. The bitter truth was that we no longer had it, we no longer believed we were invincible. Our faith in ourselves was no longer there.

Mr. Mack was the chief sufferer. Philadelphia had loyally supported us in '29 and '30. Attendance had dropped off slightly in '31 as fans said, "What's the use of watching 'em when we know they're going to win." In late '32 they said, "What's the use of watching 'em when they're out of the race?" The result was disastrous to an owner who had raised salaries all along the line before the season started. Pennsylvania's blue laws didn't help, either. Shibe Park was deserted on Sundays, the best day in the week for other clubs.

Our final road trip of the '32 season was to Washington. I sat with Mr. Mack on the train which took us back to Philadelphia. I could sense from his attitude and the silence in the car that this might be the last trip for some of us. I mentioned a recent story in a Philadelphia newspaper which had hinted that he was planning to break up the great old team.

"Don't worry about what the papers say," he assured me. "You'll be with me next year."

I went to New York with my wife for the World Series between the Yankees and the Cubs. The evening before the opening game we had a pleasant time at a performance of *Of Thee I Sing.* We were talking about the show when our taxi delivered us to the Almanac Hotel where we were staying. George Earnshaw was standing in the lobby, a tabloid newspaper in his hand.

"Take a look at this, Jim," he said, thrusting the paper at me.

I stared at the headline:

SIMMONS, HAAS AND DYKES SOLD TO WHITE SOX

I was speechless. It was impossible to believe. Just then Jimmy Colson, a Philadelphia baseball writer, burst up with a question about my reaction to the deal. "I know nothing about it," I gulped. "But it's got to be true."

Mr. Mack and his wife were crossing the lobby. I excused myself and hurried after him. "Am I going to the White Sox?" I demanded.

He looked up. "Yes, Jimmie. I've sold you to Chicago."

I turned on my heel and rejoined my wife. I was burning with indignation. Only a few days earlier Mr. Mack had assured me that I would be with the Athletics in '33. I had spent my baseball life in Philadelphia, my home town. The Athletics were my home team; every game I'd played had been for the home folks. Chicago was not for me!

Moreover, around the league the White Sox were known as a tightfisted outfit, a collection of also-rans who hadn't been in the first division since the Black Sox had sold out to gamblers in 1919. I didn't sleep that night. In the morning I came to a decision and made it vocal. I was through! I'd never go to Chicago! I watched the Series games through a fog of anger and disillusionment.

As time passed I told the world that Jimmie Dykes was retiring from baseball. I had bought a bowling alley with my Series shares and could afford to quit the game. It would be a bitter ending to my career of faithful loyalty to Mr. Mack. I resolved never to speak to him again.

One winter morning I was in the vicinity of Shibe Park and decided to drop in to say good-bye to my old friends, the clubhouse attendants. No sooner was I in the clubhouse than the door opened. Mr. Mack stood there. "Jimmie, I want to talk to you," he said. "Come on upstairs."

A few minutes later I sat in his familiar office listening to the familiar voice of the man whom I had admired since I was a brash twenty-year-old.

"I owe you an explanation, Jimmie," he began. "Last August I offered Simmons and Haas to the White Sox. They were interested, but in the course of our talks they insisted on having you as well. I turned them down. The deal was apparently dead.

"On the day before the Series I ran into Harry Grabiner in the press room at the Roosevelt Hotel. His first words were, 'I'll raise the price to one hundred and fifty thousand dollars for Simmons and Haas if you'll toss in Dykes.' This was twice as much as I'd asked for the other two boys. By the time last season was over, the Athletics were deep in debt. I had no choice. To save the club I had to let you go. I want to repeat what I told you on the train from Washington. At that time I had every intention of keeping you next year."

I understood. I told him so. Peace was restored between us before I left the room. Nevertheless, I was not convinced that I should report to the White Sox. For a month I wavered. Late in January I happened on Eddie Collins and asked his advice. "You've never met Harry Grabiner, have you?" he asked.

"No. I only know that he runs the Sox and is a cheapskate."

"Harry's one of the squarest shooters in baseball, Jimmie. Go to Pasadena. Get into shape. Keep your mouth shut. If you're of the same opinion about Harry one month later, pack your bags and go home."

It seemed like good advice. I had faith in Eddie. I took a train to Pasadena.

In a suite in a Los Angeles hotel I met Harry Grabiner and J. Louis Comiskey, the huge, 350-pound owner of the White Sox, who was resting his great bulk on a lounge. After the preliminaries of courtesy were over I went straight to the point. "I'm here to talk contract," I said.

"We know that your salary was $13,000 last year," said Mr. Grabiner. "Unfortunately we're not as prosperous as Mr. Mack's Athletics. The highest salary on the White Sox will be yours."

"And how high is that?"

"Ten thousand."

"Then I'd better grab the next train back east to Philadelphia. I can't afford to take a cut. My expenses will be higher in Chicago. And I don't think I deserve a cut."

They came back at me with strong arguments. The Sox had been founded in 1901 by Charles Comiskey, the famous Old Roman, who had died in 1931. The club had prospered until 1920 when, as a result of the Black Sox scandal, Commissioner Landis had suspended many of its stars for life. The fans had deserted the Sox, who would have foundered but for Mr. Grabiner's handling of finances. He had scraped the bottom of the cashbox to buy Simmons, Haas and me. Now, for the first time in thirteen years, the Sox would be strong enough to get into contention and win back the fans lost to the Cubs.

They pleaded with me to accept their terms. In another year, said Mr. Grabiner, they'd be able to pay me what I deserved. I was obdurate. I, too, had financial problems. I hadn't traveled across the continent to help the Sox out of theirs. I had come to play the kind of ball I'd always played, winning ball ——

A voice from the lounge interrupted me. "We want you to be happy," said Mr. Comiskey. "Your salary will be thirteen thousand, not ten."

My second career began.

We three ex-Athletics were the focus of attention as the '33 season began. Neither the passage of time nor the change in locale seemed to have slowed us down. Simmons hit .327 that season, Haas .289 and, although I was thirty-seven, I batted .260 in 153 games. Each of us was within a few points of our previous averages.

But three players do not make a ball club. The Sox were weak in the box and lacked a seasoned infield. Our shortstop was young Luke Appling, who rapped out hits at a .300 pace but who still hadn't learned how to handle tough ground balls. I coached him from spring training into the season, yelling advice to him as grounders came his way. By midsummer he had greatly improved. It was a pleasant year—we moved up one notch from sixth place. I liked Chicago and made many new friends.

These new friends unexpectedly gave me the greatest thrill of my life. That June the readers of the Chicago *Tribune* began to ballot for members of the National and American League teams who would meet in baseball's first All-Star Game in July as a feature of the Chicago World's Fair. That I could be elected to the American League team was farthest from my mind. My best years were behind me; I'd been discarded by the Athletics, my future was uncertain. But as I read the standings of candidates for the third-base spot my name steadily rose to the top and when the balloting ended I was on the squad.

So there I was on the great day, once again under

Connie Mack's management, sitting on the bench beside Ruth, Gehrig, Foxx, Grove, Simmons and other great stars. And running out to my position as Lefty Gomez took the mound against John J. McGraw's heroes of the other league.

I was batting seventh and didn't come up until one was out in the second inning. Wild Bill Hallahan was really wild and I worked a pass off him. A sacrifice put me on second. I dawdled off the bag. Lefty Gomez was at the plate. The chances of his driving me home were a million to one what with Hallahan throwing bullets and Lefty lucky if he got two hits a season. But, to my amazement, he poked a blooper into center field and I set sail, all flags flying, sliding into the plate ahead of the throw with the first run of the game.

I'd read a story which said that Mr. Mack would take me out after the third inning and put Jimmy Foxx in my place. I brought my glove to the bench and asked if I was through for the day. "Stay in there, Jimmie," he said. "You're doing all right."

So I played the entire nine innings, saw the Babe smack one of those home runs he'd always come through with in a big game, and was again behind Lefty Grove as he closed out the National leaguers in the final three innings. I had a single to cherish in my hit column as the game ended in a 4 to 2 victory for me and my mates.

It was like being king for a day.

We Sox stumbled from the start of the '34 campaign, losing 20 of our first 30 games. In May we returned from a disastrous road trip and played to such a small crowd in Comiskey Park that I could count their noses from the dugout.

That night Lou Comiskey telephoned, asking me to come to his hotel.

I was surprised when he greeted me at the door, for he spent most of his time in bed at his home or in a hospital where he was either on a special diet or recuperating from one of the many operations he underwent to determine the cause of his obesity.

As soon as I was seated he popped a stunning question:

"Jim, how would you like to manage the White Sox?"

I was utterly unprepared to answer. I'd never thought of managing, even when Chicago writers had hinted, at the time I joined the club, that I would be groomed for the post. And what was wrong with Lew Fonseca's managing? Lew was young, he knew baseball, and the sad showing of the club was not his fault —and besides, I'd become attached to him during my year with the team.

I stalled. "If you're asking for a point of information, Mr. Comiskey," I said. "I have nothing to say."

"Let's put it this way," he countered; "if you won't take the job I'll give it to someone else."

In other words, Fonseca was out, no matter how I replied. "Is this final, sir?"

"It is."

"Give me a moment to think ——"

"Of course."

For thirteen years I'd observed Mr. Mack's methods, in adversity as well as in triumph. I knew the management routine. I knew baseball. The Sox were a bad last; I'd have to pull them up by the bootstraps.

I'd never failed to accept a challenge. This was the biggest challenge of them all.

"Very well, Mr. Comiskey," I said. "I'll take the job."

I arrived at Comiskey Park the next morning, wondering what sort of a day I was in for. Apparently no one but myself knew what had happened. Lew Fonseca went about his usual duties. He called a meeting to discuss how to play the Senators in the series beginning that day. At its conclusion he gave a brief pep talk, ending with these ironic words: "We've got to get going during this home stand. If we don't, someone's going to get sacked—and it might be me."

Only I knew that he was already sacked. My tongue was tied pending an announcement from Mr. Comiskey. I felt like a heel as the game proceeded. Afterwards, Fonseca's phone rang. An hour later I was officially the manager of the White Sox.

My managerial career began the next day. I sat in the manager's office, conferred with my coaches, made out the lineup, talked to the writers, carried the lineup to the pregame parley at the plate, then took my usual place at third base. Yesterday I'd been one of nine players; now every eye was on me. I was responsible for every move the Sox made. I was the leader of a lost legion. My job was to guide it out of the wilderness. And not get lost myself.

An inexperienced manager has to learn from hard experience. I made mistakes from the first day. These were not errors in the actual play of the game. They were mistakes of judgment. Fortunately I had an owner and general manager who had confidence in me. They interfered in no way with my decisions regarding the use of players and never criticized my mistakes.

Then there are the manager's problems in human relations. Each player has his own goals, his own personal quirks. On my first trip to Philadelphia I dropped into Connie Mack's office. In the course of our long chat he gave me advice which I've never forgotten. "You're just one of the twenty-five players on the team," he said. "The only difference between you and the others is that you have authority. Let them question your judgment but never let them doubt your authority."

Like Mr. Mack I managed with a light hand but I always made my authority felt. I didn't take myself seriously. After our terrible start we were doomed to finish in last place. But I encouraged the players in the belief that better times were coming by kidding with them, kidding with the newspapermen, keeping smiles as much a part of my daily duties as deciding whether I should call for a sacrifice or a hit-and-run.

It's my belief that a manager of a major-league club should have had training in the minors. He has to test his reactions to problems as they arise. Anyone who manages in the majors must know the ordinary moves to make. The sixteen managers then—there are twenty now—were absolutely equal in their knowledge of what to do during a game. The performance a manager gets from his players depends on their ability and their response to his leadership. You've got to have the cards to win the game.

My worst mistake in those early years was impatience with faltering pitchers. I was too quick on the trigger in removing those who got into jams. A pitcher loses self-confidence when he's not permitted to ride out a storm. Unless he's noticeably tired or was obviously jittery he deserved the chance to stay in.

I resolved never to make the same mistake twice.

This meant that I studied my own moves, and when they failed I tried to find out why.

A starting pitcher told me that he was tiring although he'd been pitching shutout ball and had a 2 to 0 lead in the sixth inning. I ordered our ace reliefer, Clint Brown, to warm up. In our turn at bat we poured it on for six runs.

When the inning was over the starter picked up his glove and started for the mound. I called him back.

"Heck, I can hold an eight-run lead," he protested.

"You were tired when you were two runs ahead. You're just as tired with eight."

Brown went in and preserved the shutout.

I learned never to let a pitcher talk me out of removing him. "I can get this next man out," they'd say.

"Give me the ball," I'd order. "You're through."

Bill Dietrich didn't give me the ball. He was a cocky right-hander with lots of guts. He wound up and flung the ball over the grandstand roof. "That's the best throw you've made today," I said. "It's costing you a hundred bucks."

I never collected the fine. I collected just three fines in my long managerial career, and those were for violations of training rules. After two days of incessant rain in New York I decided that the boys might be getting restless. That midnight I posted myself in the hotel lobby to check on wayfarers. Three of my Sox had failed to be in bed by then.

Toward 2:30 two tottered in, turning pale as they saw me. They approached, excuses at the ready. I cut them short. "Don't waste your breath!" I snapped. "You're out five hundred each."

I got up and went to bed without waiting for the third delinquent.

I sent for him the following morning. "What time did you get in last night?" I asked.

"I was in bed by midnight," he lied.

"In whose bed?"

He turned red.

"That lie will cost you five hundred," I decreed.

All three of the miscreants were married men. I didn't report their fines to Mr. Grabiner. I didn't have to. My threat sufficed to make them respond religiously to the coach's knock when he made the round for midnight bedchecks on the road. On the season's last day all three came to me to wish me an affectionate farewell.

The following year I discovered that four of my players were habitually violating the midnight curfew on the road. I called a clubhouse meeting. In my hand was a mimeographed letter.

"I'm posting a copy of this letter on the bulletin board," I announced. "It's going to your wives. 'Dear Madam,' it reads, 'will you kindly let me know where your husband goes after midnight on the road? Thus far I've been unable to find out who he spends his time with. I don't want to have him trailed. I don't want to fine him as I know you need the money. If you get this information, please rush it to me. (*Signed*) Jimmie Dykes.' Any questions?"

There were none.

One infielder approached me after the meeting. "Mr. Dykes, if you ever catch me out after midnight again, fine me as much as you please. But please don't send that letter to my wife or you won't have a second baseman any more."

"I'm no home wrecker," I said. "That responsibility is yours."

The Sox were the best-behaved team in baseball the rest of the year.

The phone bell roused me from sleep in a Boston hotel one morning, at three o'clock. "Do you know where one of your players is right now?" asked a voice strange to me.

I waited.

"Well, you better come and get him ——"

"Where is he?"

"Leaning against Kelley's Bar in Scollay Square."

I sat up. "What's his name?" He told me. "Who's with him?"

"Three or four other Sox I don't recognize."

I collared the first offender the next morning. "How many drinks did you have in Kelley's last night?"

He almost collapsed. "J-just a few beers," he stammered.

A little later I saw him in the clubhouse in conference with the three other stayouts. A coach later repeated the conversation he'd overheard. "A perfect crime, huh?" said the first wayfarer. "Dykes was in bed, was he?" moaned another. "I told you we were being followed," said the third. "That guy's got eyes in the back of his head," said the fourth.

I took no action against the thirsty quartet. I let them stew in their own brew. It was my first but not my last tip from one of the many informers who hang out in bars, recognizing athletes and turning them in to their managers. My vagrant four took no more chances. They were safely tucked between sheets at midnight from then on.

Life in our dugout was free and easy. We needled, jockeyed, corrected umpires' decisions, made our voices heard. But I maintained my authority over every man on the squad—except once.

A burly righthander filled the bases in an early inning. The opposing team's cleanup hitter was coming up and I hurried to the mound. "Keep the ball low and away from this lug," I told him. "Try to make him hit it on the ground. We may get out of this with a double play."

No sooner was I back on the bench than I saw the pitcher throw a waist-high fast ball. Crack! The drive knocked a slat out of the right-field fence. It was a base-cleaning triple.

I was boiling by the time the side was retired. I let my pitcher have it.

"I'd like to see you do better!" he retorted.

"Go take a shower," I ordered. "You're through for the day."

"If you'd kept away I'd a got out of that jam," he argued. Whereupon he fired a challenge both to my judgment and authority. "What do you know about pitching, anyhow?"

My back was up. I let him talk until he used a personal epithet.

"That'll cost you fifty!" I snapped. "To the clubhouse at once!"

He stood firm, fists clenched, towering over me. "We'll settle this outside!" he challenged.

"I'll see you after the game," I promised, and added a few swear words of my own.

He darted into the runway and disappeared.

I am five feet nine. The rebel was six feet two or three. I weighed 186. He was at least 40 pounds heavier. I spent the rest of the game wondering how I'd be able to chastise a player who'd defied me before the rest of the team. It would never do for me to be whipped by one of my players.

The game ended. I joined the others as they filed into the runway. I searched for my opponent in the clubhouse. He sat, dressed for the street, on a stool before his locker. He sprang to his feet as he saw me. He was on his way, drawing nearer. His hand was raised.

"Skipper, let's shake," he said. "I'm awfully sorry. Made a fool of myself today. Let's forget it, will ya?"

I sighed with relief as I grasped his hand. I'd won a big decision without striking a blow.

We rose to fifth in '35 and to the giddy heights of third place in '36. I continued to play in every game. I was as active as ever; I hit .288 in '36 and used myself as a utility infielder, filling in at first, second and third. I celebrated my fortieth birthday in the pink of condition, thanks to my abstemious habits and my off-season exercise on bowling alleys and golf links.

We profited that year from the sensational hitting of Luke Appling. Luke led the league with a batting average of .388. He was a natural hitter to all fields and especially expert in the hit-and-run play. He'd been an unsteady fielder in his early years. Now he was as smooth as silk, a star in the field as well as with the bat.

"Old Aches and Pains," we called him. Luke was a moaner about his feeble health and battered body. In the clubhouse he was known as "Libby Holman" because he was always singing the blues. "The first time you say nothing's wrong with you," I quipped, "I'll know you're really sick." One morning he lay writhing on the rubbing table while the trainer examined his bruises. "I'm benching you today," I told him.

"No, no," he protested. "If I'm going to die I'll die in harness!"

He played that day. He cracked out two singles, a double and a triple, 4 for 4 by a "dying" man.

Luke had the habit of clicking fouls until he either worked a pass or got a pitch he could hit. That week he asked Harry Grabiner for a dozen new balls to give to his friends, and busy Harry had failed to come across with them. In batting practice Luke shot foul after foul onto the stands. "You're wasting an awful lot of balls," I kidded him.

"Just getting even with Mr. Grabiner," he replied.

Taft Wright, our tubby outfielder, batted ahead of Luke in the lineup. Tubby had a lot of trouble with signs, especially with Luke's hit-and-run sign. He made several false starts from first base one day before they finally got together and Luke singled him to third.

Afterwards I tried to get them to agree on a simple sign that Tubby could read easily. "It's not my fault," he said. "Luke mixes me up by tapping once, sometimes twice or three times with his bat on the plate. Then he'll rub the sign off and start it again."

"Suppose you make up a sign for Luke," I said. "You two look like bushers, fiddling around the way you do."

The next day Taft excitedly told me: "I've got a hit-and-run sign that Luke can't miss."

"You mean you'll give the sign, not him?"

"Why not?"

"Okay," said Luke. "What'll it be?"

"When I start to run you hit."

Luke's pivot partner was Jackie Hayes, a slick second sacker. They led the league in double plays for three straight years. One spring Hayes complained of an irritation in his right eye. Our trainer suspected that he'd gotten some Arizona dust into it and sent him to a Phoenix ophthalmologist. It wasn't dust; it was the first stage of a rare disease which eventually spread to his left eye and resulted in total blindness. In recent years he became treasurer of the Alabama county in which he resides.

In 1950, when Luke's distinguished career was drawing to a close Jackie came to Cleveland to play in a golf tournament for the blind, and visited his old pivot partner at Municipal Stadium.

"I'll challenge you to a round of golf if you'll play by my rules," he said.

Luke looked astonished. "What are your rules?"

"There's only one that matters. The game must be played at night."

The stalwart of our pitching staff was Ted Lyons, who had won more than 20 games three times in the 1920's, a remarkable performance on a consistently second-division team. Ted's aversion to defeat was almost as fierce as Lefty Grove's. I made him our Sunday pitcher because I could always depend on him to turn in a neat game before a large crowd.

Ted was the perfect gentleman in sports, the perfect athlete, always in fine fettle. In 1942, when he was forty-two years old, he won 14 games, then passed the Army's physical examination and became a captain, serving until the end of the war. He returned to the Sox in 1946 at the advanced baseball age of forty-six.

In one of his first postwar appearances he faced Ted Williams, who'd been a lieutenant in the Air Force. I saw them laughing the first time Williams came up, and I asked Lyons why afterwards.

"Where would you like me to put the ball, Lieutenant?" Lyons had asked as Williams came up.

"Is this an official request, Captain?"

"It certainly is."

Williams held his bat at waist level. "Right here."

"Very well, sir."

The ball came in at waist level. Williams was laughing so hard he couldn't swing.

Ted was the only pitcher who could talk me out of removing him. He was losing, 5 to 2, to the Yankees when I went to the mound. "I can't do worse than anyone else," he said. "The Yanks are going to win, the score'll be 7 to 4 at the finish. Let me stay in."

He was right. Precisely as Ted had predicted, the final score was New York 7, Chicago 4.

The White Sox and Cleveland Indians were embroiled in an overtime contest in 1940. A Tribe runner was on third, another on second, one out, and Ray Mack at the plate. I suddenly decided to talk to Lyons, who was pitching. "How about putting this guy on and going for the double play?" I asked.

Ted shook his head. "I'll pitch to Mack. I'll make him hit." I didn't think much of that idea but I said, "Okay," and returned to the bench. Mack promptly singled through the drawn-in infield. The game was over, we were defeated. As the players trudged across the field I caught up with Ted. "You sure made him hit all right," I growled.

"You're the boss from now on," Ted said.

It was the last time I ever let him talk me out of yanking him.

On another day Ted pitched all but perfect ball against the Boston Red Sox for eight innings and was leading, 2 to 0. Boob McNair, our second baseman, grabbed a grounder, then flung it into the dirt past Joe Kuhel at first base. A runner on second scored, the batter reached second. On the next play Boob made a sensational backhand scoop of a drive into the hole, then fired it a mile over Kuhel's head.

With the score tied, Ted hitched up his pants and retired the side on strikes. He set the Red Sox down one-two-three until the twelfth inning. Then Ted Williams swung and the ball was pocketed by a bleacherite.

Lyons bolted from the field, stormed into the clubhouse, kicked his locker, tossed his gear around. He showered, dressed without a word, and headed for parts unknown.

The next day, no Lyons. At eleven o'clock the following morning he entered the clubhouse. I had no private office at Fenway Park; my headquarters were in a corner of the locker room. I saw him approach. "Don't tell me where you were yesterday," I said. "I'd have been with you if I was a drinking man."

Both Ted and Luke have been honored by election to the Hall of Fame.

For four years I tried to make Zeke Bonura realize that a first baseman must be more than a fixed target for throws. Zeke was a powerful hitter; he had quick hands that could dig balls out of the turf whenever they came directly at him, but he was unable to use his feet except for standing. "Why didn't you go after that ball?" I asked when an easy grounder skipped past him into right field.

"Couldn't get to it, Poppa," he replied, using his personal pet name for me.

I turned to Coach Luke Sewell. "Couldn't that ball be handled?"

"By Bonura? No. By any other first baseman? Yes."

Zeke was a pepperpot, a big ray of sunshine to his mates. He cheered them—or himself—whenever an ordinary play was executed . . . and sometimes when it wasn't.

In one game, a batter sent a dribbler to Zeke with the bases full and two out. Zeke moved toward it with the enthusiasm and doubt of a man pursuing a cake of soap in a bathtub. He squeezed it. It popped out of his hands. He pounced on it. It ducked away. Then he caught up with it and kicked it. Meanwhile runners were chasing each other around the bases while big Zeke was trying to surround the elusive pill.

Finally he pinned it to earth, looked up and saw a runner scampering to third. Zeke threw with more force than direction. The ball went toward third and over my head. The last of four runs scored.

Undaunted by these monumental errors, Zeke tried to reassure our stunned pitcher. "Thassaway, fellow!" he chirped. "Stick in there, kid!"

Another day the Sox were leading Washington by one run with two out in the ninth inning when Rocky Stone, the Senators' speedy outfielder, hit the ball to Zeke's right. Jackie Hayes could have handled the routine out easily, but for reasons unknown Zeke darted in front of Jackie, made a glittering backhand stop, then stumbled as he threw to Ted Lyons, who was covering first. Stone, of course, beat the throw. Zeke was so proud of his rare fielding feat that he raised his arm and gave the Mussolini salute. A single put Stone on third but Lyons bore down and struck out the final Senator.

"What's the idea of that Mussolini salute?" I demanded when I encountered Zeke in the locker room. "Next time you give that Mussolini salute make sure the batter's a Fascist, will you?"

"Aw, Poppa, I didn't know. And what's a Fascist, anyhow? That's a new word to me."

Zeke never bothered with such trivial things as signs. Appling doubled with none out in a late inning of a close game. I gave my third-base coach, Billy Webb, the bunt sign. Webb relayed it to Zeke. He stepped out of the batter's box and scratched his head, then stared at Webb, who repeated the sign. Zeke continued to stare. Webb tried again. Zeke looked imploringly at the coach.

I climbed the dugout steps. "Bunt, ya meathead!" I yelled. No reaction. "B-u-n-t, bunt! Get it?"

Zeke woke up. He laid down a perfect sacrifice. I lay down on the bench and sobbed.

Zeke contributed to the merriment of life on the Sox. I hated to part with him but when the opportunity to trade him arose I sent him to Washington for Joe Kuhel, a much more mobile first baseman. When the Senators rolled into Chicago for the first time during the 1938 season Coach Bing Miller reminded me that Zeke knew our signs.

"He didn't know 'em when he was with us. Why should we change 'em now?" I asked.

Zeke reached third base during that day's game. Between pitches he stole a glance at our dugout. Just then a mosquito landed on my nose. I waved it off with the scorecard I was holding. Waving a scorecard was my sign for a steal. As the pitcher wound up Zeke edged down the base path. With the delivery he crash-bombed into the plate with such impact that he bowled over our catcher. "Safe!" proclaimed the umpire.

Zeke had stolen home on one of our signs!

But the next time up Zeke performed in his peculiar Zeke-ish fashion. He rammed a clean single to center. Chicago fans loudly cheered their old favorite. He stepped off first base, doffed his cap and bowed low. Catcher Luke Sewell promptly fired the ball to Joe Kuhel. At the glorious moment of public acclaim Zeke was ignobly picked off.

Nothing gripes a manager more than a missed sign. We were locked in an extra-inning game when Bob Feller began to pitch relief for Cleveland. Feller was notoriously wild in his early years and I told my hitters to wait him out. Two of them waited and were walked. Tubby Wright was up.

Wright took two wide balls. Mule Haas was coaching at third. I flashed him the take sign and he relayed it to Wright.

A moment later . . . craaackk! The ball was up, up, up and over the right-field wall. Wright was grinning on his way around the bases. He came grinning into the dugout, looking for congratulations.

I put on my most serious face. "Tubby . . . come here!"

"Here I am," he cheerfully sang.

"What's the take sign?"

"The coach brushes his letters."

"Didn't you see Haas give it?"

"Aw, Skipper, I wasn't looking to take. I was looking for a fast ball—and there it was, right over the dish ——"

"And you swung?"

"Do I get fined for hitting a home run?"

I broke up. "Not by this manager, you old son of a gun!"

Dealing in ballplayers, buying, selling, trading, is dealing in human lives. Lou Comiskey and Harry Grabiner gave me the right to initiate and complete deals. All they asked was that I notify them when a deal was consummated.

I'll never forget the expression on Al Simmons' face when he walked into a Detroit hotel room and heard me say that he'd been sold to the Tigers.

"For how much?" he asked, and I knew how he felt, that he was used goods, marked down.

"Seventy-five thousand."

His eyes lighted up. "It's nice to know that I'm worth that much," said the star who ranks as the greatest right-hand hitter of all time in my book.

The best time to make a deal is during the major and minor league meetings when everyone in baseball is under one hotel roof. Everyone has scanned scouting reports and waiver lists. Everyone is trying to improve his team at everyone else's expense.

Any time two heads are seen together baseball writers cook up a mythical deal. I began a discussion with Casey Stengel, who was then managing the Boston Braves, with the intention of inducing him to let me have a Brave infielder. Casey talked for five hours nonstop and I never got the chance to mention the man I had in mind. At 1 A.M. I'd had it and I went to bed. For once I'd been out-talked.

Most deals are made by general managers after consultation with the field manager. I was on my own. Unlike some dealers, I never made a practice of running down the ability of a ballplayer I wanted. I kept my cards above the table. In 1936 I set my cap for Thornton Lee, then a young relief specialist with Cleveland. To get him I had to arrange an intricate three-sided deal with Washington that took weeks of conversation and involved five other players. It was one of the best deals I ever made, for Lee became a bulwark of the White Sox staff, winning 22 games for us in 1941 and continuing on the firing line until 1947.

I was even happier about a deal I never made. In 1951 when I was managing the Athletics George M. Weiss of the Yankees asked me if I was willing to trade Bobby Shantz. I was decidedly in the market for a lively infielder or a good-hitting outfielder and when Weiss mentioned Gerry Coleman, Billy Martin or Hank Bauer as possible counters I welcomed the idea.

The Athletics were going nowhere that spring and I had seldom used little Shantzie. A few days later Weiss notified me that the deal was off. Shortly afterwards I put Shantzie into starting rotation. He won 18 games that season and a sensational 24 in 1952, including some beautiful performances against the Yankees.

I didn't know why Weiss had gone cold on the deal until I encountered Casey Stengel at a pregame conference. "Thanks for not grabbing Bobby Shantz," I said.

"He sure beats us." grumbled Case'.

"Why didn't Weiss take him when he had the chance?"

"He thought something was wrong with his arm because you weren't using him."

Shantzie's career as a starter ended when his left wrist was hit by a pitched ball. He eventually became

a Yankee reliefer and led the league in earned run
averages in 1957.

It was a rare mistake of judgment by the Yankees,
the best-hated team in the league. Yankee-hating has
gone out of style since the ex-Bombers faded in recent
years. It was the popular pastime of the other seven
clubs in the league from my earliest days, when they
stomped all over us Athletics. I continued to hate them
as they continued to rub the White Sox into the dirt
in later years.

I didn't hate the Yankee players. They were the best.
I hated the cold arrogance of the Yankee organization
for crucifying us weak little guys who couldn't defend
ourselves against the big brutes it sent in against us.
Whenever we were scheduled to meet the Yankees I'd
tell my players "Let's beat these guys in this series if
it's the last thing we do." My record against the Yankees is close to .500 as a result of my steaming up the
White Sox to put extra effort into their play against
them.

Once we took the first three games of a four-game
series at the Yankee Stadium. When Joe McCarthy
showed his face before the fourth game I led my boys
in taunting him: "What's the matter, Joe? Afraid to
show up today? Wanta call off the game?" Joe said
nothing. He didn't have to. His team kicked the heck
out of us by something like 11 to 1 that day.

I must admit that I secretly admired the Yankees,
from Ed Barrow down to the batboy. I especially admired Barrow's three great scouts, Paul Krichell, Joe
Devine and Bill Essick. It was they who unearthed the
brilliant stars who licked us and everyone else. I admired Ed Barrow for having developed them and for

bolstering their pride in wearing the pinstriped uniform.

Barrow surrounded himself with the best baseball men in the game. After his retirement the Yankees continued to win under Weiss, thanks to the organization Barrow had founded. Now, years later, the stream of talent has dried up. The Yankee Terror has ended.

I had one victory over the Yankees that never appeared in the league standings. On a rainy day I went down to the Stevens brothers' kitchen in Yankee Stadium for a sandwich and coffee and found Mr. Barrow there. "If today's game is called," I said, "We'll reschedule it for later in the season. The Sox will leave New York this afternoon."

"You have an off-day tomorrow," he said. "We'll play the game then."

"We have a doubleheader the day after tomorrow. My boys need the off-day for rest."

"I don't care what your team needs. You can stay in New York overnight and ——"

"No, we won't! I've already made arrangements for space on the train leaving at five—and we're going!"

We were locked, horns to horns, in mortal combat. I broke it off: "Let the American League decide. I'll call the president's office ——"

"No, you won't," he growled. "I'll make the call."

Which he did. He returned a few minutes later with a half grin on his face. "You win," he conceded, "but ——"

And he stunned me by saying, "You're staying here until four o'clock to see if the rain stops and we can play today."

The rain didn't stop.

During the Cardinal-Red Sox World Series in 1946 I encountered Barrow in Boston's Copley Plaza Hotel. "You and Larry MacPhail would make a good combination for the Yankees next year," he said. "Both of you would be battling for top publicity and you'd handle the team right." Joe McCarthy had quit the Yankees earlier that year; I had resigned as manager of Hollywood. It was a high compliment from the game's most successful operator. "We're going to pick a manager at French Lick after the Series. With your permission I plan to recommend you strongly for the job."

"I appreciate that very much," I said.

A few days after the Cards had beaten the Red Sox a telegram came:

SORRY BUT BUCKY HARRIS IS NEW MANAGER OF THE
YANKEES.   BARROW

Two years later Harris was out. I was again under consideration but Casey Stengel won the prize.

In 1937 the White Sox had repeated their third-place finish of the previous year and I was having delusions of grandeur, but we lapsed to sixth in 1938. I reduced myself to occasional utility service. I was like an old firehorse that stirs when any bell rings.

In the spring of 1939 I was approaching my forty-third year. I could still hit, but the old legs and old reactions weren't what they used to be. In a game with the Yankees I went back for a pop fly and fell flat on my fanny, a most embarrassing moment.

On June 14, the eve of cut-down day, Harry Grabiner got me on the phone. "Who are you cutting tomorrow?"

"I've got his name right here," I said. "It's Dykes . . . D-y-k-e-s."

"What: You're quitting?"

"My legs are gone, Harry, I'm through."

It's hard to break a lifelong habit. A year was to pass before I became accustomed to managing from the bench. It was hard to resist grabbing a bat when a pinch hit was needed. For twenty-two years I'd been in the game. Now I was out.

It was a gratifying year. The Sox were fourth the day I released myself and in fourth place at the season's end. They played interesting, hustling ball. Chicago fans increasingly supported us.

A great change was taking place in baseball. The first night game in Chicago had been played in August 1938, two weeks after Lou Comiskey's death. It was a pity that Lou had not lived to see the capacity night crowds, the many women who attended after dark. Games under the lights promised to relieve the financial stress which had forced the club to borrow half a million dollars from the First National Bank of Chicago. I had hopes of liquidating this debt, of organizing a farm system and even of having enough ready cash to buy players.

The new president of the club was Mrs. Grace Comiskey, Lou's widow, Harry Grabiner remaining as vice-president and general manager. Mrs. Comiskey promised to participate more actively in club affairs than her husband had. My own position was secure; I'd been given public credit for improving the standing of a team which operated on a short bankroll.

But there were subtle differences from the old regime. One day while I was engaged in a wordy controversy with umpire John Quinn I felt a hot breath on my neck.

"Who the heck is this?" demanded Quinn.

I turned around. A tall, skinny kid in a White Sox uniform was at my elbow. "Meet Mr. Charles Comiskey, Mr. Quinn," I said. "Mr. Comiskey is going to own the Sox one day."

"I don't care if he owns the Tribune Tower right now!" said His Majesty, the ump. "Get him off the field!"

Chuck Comiskey retreated. He was fifteen then and had shown up in our dugout wearing a Sox uniform, ostensibly to learn what happens during a ball game as seen from the bench. Ted Lyons had kidded him into joining me in my argument with Quinn, telling him he had the right to go where he pleased in the ball park named after his famous grandfather.

The consequences of Chuck's temerity were revealed when I received notification from President Harridge of the American League that all but authorized personnel were barred from the dugout and field during games. Mr. Harridge forgot to fine me for using bad language in the presence of a minor.

Mrs. Comiskey did not restrict my independence as manager or my right to make deals. However, she sat in a field box during home games and sometimes made her presence uncomfortably felt. During a Mother's Day doubleheader, Orval Grove, my starter, suffered a mild wild spell early in the first game. Mrs. Comiskey stood up among the women fans who were her guests and made an attempt to catch my attention. When she failed, she showed by gestures that she wanted Grove to be removed. I had confidence in Orval and let him stay in the box. He regained control and eventually was the winner.

Between games I went on the radio. On my return I stopped at Mrs. Comiskey's box. "Madam," I said,

"I am managing this team and need no advice about when to remove a pitcher. And fans and the press need no reminder that you are president of the club."

She was taken aback, and promised: "I won't do it again, Mr. Dykes."

We finished in a tie for fourth in 1940 and third in 1941. We were a small power in the American League, capable of challenging, if not overcoming, contenders.

Then, a bolt from the blue, Pearl Harbor! In 1942 we lost several of our best players to the armed services and dropped to sixth place. With 4Fs and teen-agers in the lineup we managed to reach fourth in '43, but we tumbled to seventh in '44 and sixth in '45.

The war had created a critical situation for the Sox. The bank, acting as trustee under Lou Comiskey's will, demanded that the club be sold in order to liquidate its debt, an action forced by a technicality in Illinois law. Mrs. Comiskey refused to sell.

During this period she had supplanted Harry Grabiner with Leslie O'Connor, formerly Commissioner Landis's aide. My long and harmonious association with Harry ended. I'd been Harry's man; mutual confidence had existed between us. Mr. O'Connor was an able baseball man, but I felt that instead of being dismissed, Harry deserved a gold medal for keeping the Sox afloat in stormy financial waters from the 1920's into the war years. I could read the handwriting on the wall.

Despite our low state in '45 I'd succeeded in keeping the team's morale high. We'd put up a fight for every game. We'd given the fans their money's worth. We'd talked it up, needled, jockeyed, kept umpires on their toes. I'd even installed an official needler. Karl Sheel, an ex-marine, had worked out at our Pasadena camp that spring. I'd signed him as batting practice pitcher after he'd told me that regular work might strengthen his weak back and give him a chance to make the staff as a regular. Karl had a high, strident voice. He took lessons in ribbing from me and Mule Haas, who was still my coach. He became a voice in uniform, a getter of goats.

For two days in St. Louis Karl rode the Brownies, pennant winners in the wartime league of 1944. Before the third game Ellis Clary and Sid Jakucki tried to silence him forcibly. Blows were struck. We rushed to Karl's defense; the brawl spread to our dugout. Karl was bruised in the scuffle; I received a spike wound in the arm. Jakucki's head was gashed and Clary's lip split.

It was a rough quick battle in which blows actually found their targets. I don't defend mayhem on the diamond. I do defend bench-jockeying, an old baseball tradition that has fallen into disuse in recent years.

A silent ball club is a dead ball club. The '45 Sox were very much alive. We were in the first division most of the season. But we lacked hitting and dropped below the .500 mark, finishing in sixth place.

During spring training in 1946 I fell ill. A Los Angeles physician diagnosed my ailment as abdominal adhesions and warned me that I might die unless they were quickly removed. I underwent an immediate operation.

A cold cigar—the doctor wouldn't let me light it— was my closest companion for the next few weeks. It was mid-May before I was well enough to travel to Chicago. I found the White Sox had precisely the same record as on the day in 1934 when Lou Comiskey had made me manager: 10 wins, 20 losses. We were in last place.

Mrs. Comiskey was in a flutter. Over the phone she said, "We'd have started better if you'd had your operation in Chicago."

"Dead men make poor managers," I told her. "If I'd have waited for a Chicago doctor to cut me up I'd have been ready for an autopsy, not an operation." I sensed that all was not well in our relations. "I'll be at your office tomorrow morning," I said.

The following morning I was greeted by a formidable assemblage: Mrs. Comiskey, Leslie O'Connor, Chuck, and Mrs. Comiskey's daughter, Mary Lou. It was apparent from the start that Mrs. Comiskey was in doubt about my ability to rouse the team from its doldrums. From my point of view it was important to know where I stood. The war was over, veterans were returning to the diamond, but it would take at least another year to build a winner with the material at hand for a basis. I asked that my contract be extended through the 1947 season.

Mrs. Comiskey flatly refused.

"Then pay me off and forget me," I said.

"I won't do that, either."

"Well, I'll do the best I can with the team. You'll feel happier when you fire me at the end of this season."

After a flurry of words I walked out.

The next day I was paid off on my one-year contract. My happy years of managing the White Sox were over. When I'd accepted Lou Comiskey's bid to manage I'd thought I might last for a year or two or three. Instead I'd lasted twelve. By trades or with petty cash

I'd procured many a player deemed a troublemaker by his former employer. When they reported I'd told every one of them that they were starting from scratch and that I'd forget anything that had happened before they joined the Sox. They'd responded by playing the best ball that was in them. I'd had happy, contented teams.

The closest I'd come to a pennant had been in 1936 when we'd finished third, half a game behind the Detroit Tigers. My only power hitter had been Zeke Bonura, although Joe Kuhel had hit 27 homers one year. Otherwise our idea of power was a double from the bats of Luke Appling or Taft Wright. One solid slugger might have won it all for us on several occasions. I could never obtain a slugger, with cash or by prayer.

I'd talked myself out of worrying. I'd had fun in every game. I'd had my bouts with umpires, as I shall tell later, but I'd never had one bout with myself.

I could look back on many a laugh. I'd always been one of the boys. I'd kept Connie Mack's advice in mind: to be a member of the team but never to let my authority be questioned.

I'd learned a lot about human nature. I'd eased tantrums such as Bill Dietrich pulled when he lost his head after an easy fly fell safe. I'd removed him and he came snorting to the bench, telling me what he thought of me. I'd ordered him to take his temper to the showers and cool it off. He did and later came shamefaced to me and asked me to lay him across my knee and spank him.

I'd pulled Edgar Smith out of a game and told him that his IQ was below 50 for not obeying my orders.

"You can't say that to me!" he roared.

"I'll repeat it after the game in the clubhouse," I'd told him.

When the game ended I removed my bridge. It had cost me money and I didn't want it to be broken. I went straight to Smith. "Okay, I'm here. Let's go!" I said.

"Not before I take an IQ test," he said, and we both burst out laughing.

I'd fined only two players of the scores I'd managed, and made the fines stick. I fined Johnny Whitehead for being out of shape, the one unpardonable sin in my calendar. I'd threatened to fine Jake Wade $100 but did not intend to report the fine to Harry Grabiner. Wade went around the clubhouse bragging that he'd put one over on me, that I was a softie who talked fines but never collected them. I took the hundred out of his next check.

These were rare ripples on the even surface of my years with the White Sox. I'd been my own boss, I'd put teams of my choice on the field and played them as I saw fit. If I hadn't won a pennant it was because the club didn't have the resources to create a farm system, to hire scouts who could have located a potential DiMaggio, a Williams, a Feller, a Foxx, in the bushes.

There's an old baseball saying, You can't steal first base.

Add this one, You can't steal a pennant.

5

EAST IS EAST AND WEST IS WEST

ONE WEEK LATER I was packing in preparation for a much needed vacation when the phone rang. On the wire was Bill Veeck, who asked me to meet him in Detroit to discuss important business.

Veeck was a refreshing contrast to the stodgy magnates who sat around long tables plotting how not to bring new ideas to the game. His busy brain was full of schemes which, he swore, would revolutionize baseball and spread its popular appeal into infinity. I agreed to delay my departure in order to see him.

In a restaurant off Cadillac Square he confided that

he was about to close a deal which would give him control of the Cleveland Indians.

"You've drawn a winning hand," I told him. "You'll have a million-dollar pitcher in Bob Feller. And a half million's worth of shortstopping in Lou Boudreau. Congratulations, Bill."

"Here's some other news you'll like. Harry Grabiner will be my general manager."

"A perfect choice."

"And you'll be my manager."

His mention of Harry's name had prepared me for this offer. "I can't take it, Bill," I said.

"Why not? Have you signed with someone else?"

"No, I haven't. But you already have a manager in Boudreau. If you demote him you'll have to trade him. And there's no better shortstop in the league right now."

"I won't take No for an answer, Jim," he shot back. "Think it over. We'll settle terms later." He enthusiastically outlined his plans. Baseball was on the upbeat in this postwar period when everyone needed relief from memories of the great conflict. Major changes in the game were coming. He planned to make Cleveland the capital of the baseball world. It was hard to resist his optimistic picture of things to come. He left me with the impression that he expected me to take charge of the Indians later in the month when they would come to Chicago for a series with the White Sox.

I decided to spend a few days with an intimate friend in Williamsport, Pennsylvania, before going home to my wife and children in Philadelphia. No sooner had I arrived in my friend's house than the phone rang. It was Harry Grabiner: "Bill would like to see you in Detroit. When can you come?"

"What does he want?"

"I can't tell you on the phone."

"I know what's on his mind. Tell him he'll be making a big mistake if he drops Boudreau as manager."

"It's vitally important that you tell him yourself, Jim."

"Okay, I'll come."

I arrived in Detroit on the eve of a series between the Tigers and Yankees and registered at the Fort Shelby Hotel; then I called Harry. "You're just in time," he said. "Bill and Boudreau are here in the next room."

"Tell Bill he's looking for trouble. He should wait until after this season ends before thinking about changing managers."

"I'll tell Bill what you just said, but it won't do any good. He's adamant about your taking over the team. He's concluded the purchase deal and wants to get organized."

"Let me think this over for a while, Harry. Call me back later tonight."

I wrestled with my misgivings until midnight. The Indians were far down in the race. Without Boudreau they would fall lower. I saw no way of keeping him, a former manager, on the team. Besides, I sorely needed a vacation after my operation.

The phone interrupted my thoughts. "Bill has decided that you are right, Jim," said Harry. "Boudreau will stay on as manager."

I remained in Detroit to see the opening game of the Tiger-Yankee series. As soon as I arrived in the Tiger stadium I found that the press had gotten wind of Veeck's offer to me. Nothing I could say would convince the newspapermen that Bill and I were not involved in a dark plot to unseat Boudreau. "I haven't seen Veeck since I came to Detroit and don't intend to," I told them. It was an awkward situation that mere denials failed to straighten out.

I did a lot of thinking the next day as I chased a golf ball about the fairways with Jerry Moore, manager of the Fort Shelby Hotel. I was satisfied that I'd done the right thing by turning down Veeck's offer and avoiding walking into a delicate situation on the Indians. On my return from the links I found the afternoon newspapers flooded with stories about Bill's purchase of the Indians, which included rumors that he was considering me as manager. I decided to leave for Chicago at once.

Before I could get away, Ed McCauley, dean of Cleveland's baseball writers, reached me on the phone. He refused to accept my denials of the rumors. "I am not going to Cleveland," I said. "Call me at my apartment in the Windermere Hotel in Chicago at ten tomorrow evening. If I'm not there it'll be because I'm in Cleveland with Bill Veeck. If I answer the phone, will you believe that I'm telling the truth?"

"Yes, I will," said Ed.

On the dot of ten I answered the phone. "Are you satisfied, Ed?" I asked.

Two years later Lou Boudreau went 4 for 4 in the first play-off game in American League history and then led his champion Indians to victory over the Boston Braves in the World Series. Fourteen years were to pass before, under unprecedented circumstances, I finally became manager of the Indians.

I decided to escape the big-league scene on a leisurely motor tour of the West. I paused en route to study the laws of chance on the gaming tables of Las

Vegas. Then to Hollywood for a peek at baseball as it was being played in the Pacific Coast League.

I was renewing old acquaintanceships and enjoying myself mightily until I accepted a luncheon invitation at the Brown Derby from Bob Cobb, a director of the Hollywood Stars. Between soup and dessert Cobb told me about the trials and tribulations of minor-league ball. The Stars were in fifth place and drawing poorly. Little by little Cobb approached the climax of his recital. My coming to Hollywood was fortunate, he said, both for the Stars and for me. I was a glamorous name in baseball; everyone in Southern California knew me from my annual visits to the White Sox camp in Pasadena. Put together in one package, Dykes plus the Stars would bring a sensational upturn to Hollywood baseball, both in the field and at the box office.

I was still the old firehorse, ready to leap into harness at the sound of any bell. Moreover, idleness was boring me, the climate was perfect. I found myself saying, "I like it here, Bob. I think I can get the Stars going. Yes, I'll take the job."

I was in good company. Lefty O'Doul was piloting San Francisco, Casey Stengel was at Oakland, and Jim Turner at Portland. The level of Pacific Coast ball was generally high. The Stars responded to what the newspapers called my "magic touch," which consisted of nothing more than establishing rapport between the players and myself. They spurted after I took over, lifting themselves from fifth to third, and earning a spot in the play-offs.

Our opponents in the postseason games, four out of seven to win, were O'Doul's San Franciscans, first in the regular season. We dropped the first two games to the Seals, after which I discovered that although baseball is baseball wherever it is played, it is taken somewhat less seriously in the minor leagues, even in Class AAA, than in the majors.

On the afternoon of the third play-off game I glanced into the taproom of the San Francisco hotel where we were staying. About ten of my Stars were draped about the mahogany, glasses of foaming brew before them.

I barged into their midst. "You boys have had enough," I said. "Beer before any game is out. You ought to have the sense not to lap it up before an important play-off game."

They paid up and scattered. They lost that night's game and eliminated themselves the following evening with a fourth straight defeat.

The following spring I posted an order in the clubhouse:

"Drinking of alcoholic liquor before games is forbidden. Beer will be available to all after games."

This was the unwritten law in the majors. I had to spell it out in Hollywood.

An independent minor-league club such as the Stars depended on the major-league market both for veterans on the way down and on the income from the sales of youngsters on the way up. The '47 Stars had only three players who later made good in the big leagues—Tony Lupien, Jim Delsing, and Gus Zernial. Although I lacked the authority of my White Sox years to procure players I was responsible for Zernial's coming to Hollywood.

I noticed that big Gus had hit 41 home runs in '46 with a minor-league team of low classification, and asked Oscar Reichow, the Stars' president, to put in a

draft claim for him. The claim was filed, but Cleveland
also drafted him, superseding our claim.

Early in the '47 season I read that Zernial had won a
game for the Baltimore Orioles of the International
League by blasting two mammoth home runs. Accord-
ing to baseball law a minor-league draft such as ours
went into effect when a major-league club released
a draftee without playing him. "Bill Veeck won't like
this," I said as I sent a telegram to Commissioner
Happy Chandler asking that Zernial be transferred
from Baltimore to Hollywood.

Chandler upheld my claim and Zernial became a
Star. And what a Star! He led the team in batting with
a .344 average and walloped some of the longest home
runs ever seen in the Pacific Coast League. Gus may
have swung a potent bat, but he was an uncertain
judge of fly balls. I ordered Mule Haas, who had followed me to Hollywood, to take him in hand. After
chasing hundreds of Mule's fungoes he became a tol-
erably good outfielder. In 1948 Gus led the league in
RBIs with 156 and hits with 237, among the latter 40
home runs. Leslie O'Connor phoned me that year that
he would pay $25,000 for my blaster. "Sold!" I ex-
claimed. "The Sox have got themselves a slugger at
last!"

Despite good hitting—we led the league in this department—we were unable to compete with the Angels
or Seals in 1947 and finished a disappointing sixth. We
were not competing with them in obtaining players of
quality. Oscar Reichow was less than successful in
establishing good relations with big-league executives.
Many transactions with big-league clubs are the result
of under-the-table understandings between executives.
This was known as a "gentleman's agreement," a mere

handshake over scotch and soda often confirming a deal. Oscar sometimes forgot with whom he had shaken hands.

In the fall of '47 I really went Hollywood. I became a movie actor, playing none other than myself in *The Stratton Story,* a movie based on a tragedy of real life.

Monte Stratton's effective pitching had helped put the White Sox in fourth place in 1939. Later a hunting gun had accidentally gone off, severing a vital artery in his leg which had to be amputated. Monte was the kind of fellow who wouldn't say die. He had mastered the use of an artificial leg and had rejoined the Sox as a coach. It was a moving sight to watch him sit before his locker, oiling the artificial limb and attaching it to the stump.

A Hollywood screenwriter, touring the South, happened to attend a semipro game in the small Texas town where Monte lived. A batter laid down a bunt. The pitcher stumbled as he went after it and lay on the ground in an awkward position until his teammates helped him to his feet. The writer asked questions. "Oh, that's Monte Stratton, used to pitch for the White Sox," replied a neighboring fan. "He's still quite a pitcher on only one leg."

It was true . . . Monte had quit the Sox and returned home, where his brave struggle against adversity had made him the town hero.

The screenwriter returned to Hollywood and concocted a story, part fact, part fiction, based on the tragic accident, selling it to Metro-Goldwyn-Mayer, who assigned Sam Wood, the noted director, to it. In the course of casting it Wood chose Jimmy Stewart to play the lead. I learned about it and had little difficulty in convincing him that I could play Jimmy Dykes.

So I was up at dawn each morning and reporting to the studio, studying my lines, rehearsing, advising Mr. Wood on baseball techniques and helping him round up as many of the Hollywood Stars as we could find for the diamond sequences.

I sat in my own canvas chair, my name in bold letters on the back. Jimmy Stewart amazed me by his professional form on the mound. Marv Shea, who had been Monte's catcher on the Sox, handled Jimmy's delivery. Gene Bearden, Johnny Lindell and Bill Dickey added realism as Monte's opponents.

The ballplayers took their debuts as movie actors seriously. Sam Wood directed Bill Dickey to take a third strike with the bases full. "Not me!" Bill protested. "I never took a third strike with my bat on my shoulder in real life—why should I do it here?"

I rattled off my lines like one of those Method actors, which wasn't hard, for I'd fixed them up to sound like the lingo of talkative Jimmy Dykes. *The Stratton Story* was a grand success, winning the *Photoplay Magazine* award as the best picture of 1948. I might have won an Oscar by now if I'd stayed an actor for good instead of going back to my baseball career.

I know I would have been happier if I hadn't managed the Stars in 1948. By August the team had drifted down to seventh place. That month I was summoned to the club's office for a conference. I knew what was coming. To put it bluntly—I was fired.

"You're firing the wrong man," I said. "This club needs a new president who can get new players more than it needs a new manager!"

The scene shifts from sunny California to frozen

Minnesota and the coldest winter I ever experienced. I toasted my shins in a hotel lobby among other job seekers at the Minneapolis winter meetings, where everyone worth seeing in baseball could be seen. Among the first familiar faces I saw was that of Arthur Ehlers, the genial gentleman whom Connie Mack had appointed general manager of the Athletics, a necessary appointment now that Mr. Mack was in his eighty-sixth year and no longer able to combine managing with the details of club operation.

The thought flashed through my mind—why not go back to my baseball home? "I'd like to come to Philadelphia as a coach," I told Arthur.

"The job's yours, Jim," he said, "as far as I'm concerned. But I'll have to consult Mr. Mack."

"Is he here?"

"He's upstairs in his suite."

Within an hour Arthur brought the answer: "Mr. Mack said he'd love to have you back, but he's afraid the salary will be a stumbling block."

"Not to me. I'm willing to work for less for the privilege of eating home-cooked meals with my family."

"Then let's settle it at once."

Thirty-two years had passed since I had first sat with Mr. Mack in his old-fashioned parlor while he questioned me and settled my baseball fate. His hair was whiter but his back was straight and his voice strong as we quickly came to terms.

I was again on the Athletics, again with Mr. Mack.

I'm not a sentimental guy, but I had a tingle in the vicinity of my heart as I registered in the George Washington Hotel at West Palm Beach the following spring. Mr. Mack rose from his chair in the lobby to greet me. Al Simmons, my locker-room pal of the great days, came striding toward me, hand outstretched in welcome. It was like in the good old Twenties when you and I were young, Maggie, but, alas, we're young no longer.

The next day I was out on the diamond in my clean Athletic suit. I threw batting practice. I hit grounders and lofted fungoes. I had more aches and pains that week than Luke Appling ever suffered in a season's bouts with hypochondria. I was fifty-three. The sportswriters took one look at my curves before and curves behind, and dubbed me "The Little Round Man." My only worry was that I'd get so round I couldn't see my shoes. I put on a sweatshirt in the hope of melting off my superfluous poundage. I remained round.

When exhibition games began I was first-base coach, Al Simmons giving Mr. Mack's signs off third. Mine was the easier job. I threw up the STOP sign before overzealous runners who were aiming to stretch ordinary singles into doubles. I kept an eye on sly first sackers who'd slip behind runners for pick-off throws. And I had lots of conversations with first-base umpires, mostly about their decisions. It was a lazy man's job which I could have done sitting in an easy chair.

And on the bench was the Old Man, Connie Mack, as straightbacked and alert as ever, his enthusiasm for baseball as keen as on the day I first met him. He had an assistant manager now, his son Earl Mack, the only evidence that his energies were dwindling.

The Athletics were a lively team with a tight infield, composed of Ferris Fain at first, Pete Suder at second, Eddie Joost at short and Hank Majeski at third. They had finished fourth in '48 after thirteen seasons in the second division, in nine of which they had ended in the cellar. It was a miracle that Mr. Mack had survived the years of Depression and war, that he still carried on despite old age and chronic lack of money.

I learned that he had prepared for the inevitable by distributing his stock in the club to his three sons, Earl, Roy and Connie, Jr., and to his wife. They were engaged in a factional fight to gain control after his death. Control meant little, for large sums had been borrowed from the Connecticut General Life Insurance Company and also from the Jacobs brothers, concessionaires.

The Athletics played snappy ball that year, Alex Kellner, a rookie southpaw, won twenty games. Phil Marchildon, who'd won nineteen in '47, had a sore arm which rendered him virtually useless. Barney McCoskey, until then a consistent .300 hitter, came up with a bad back which idled him all season. We flirted with second place until June, then slowly slipped into fifth.

That December Mr. Mack took a last desperate plunge in the hope of putting the team in contention. He bought third-baseman Bob Dillinger and outfielder Paul Lehner from the St. Louis Browns for $100,000 and four players. Dillinger was the key to the deal; he had hit .324 in '48 and was regarded as a fine fielder. It was a gamble that failed. In June Dillinger was sold to the Pirates for $35,000, a disastrous loss of much needed money. The team was also stricken with pitching woes. Lehner mysteriously lost his hitting knack. Two starters, Dick Fowler and Joe Coleman, were sidelined with sore arms. We lost ten straight in August. The disappointing 1950 season ended with the Athletics in last place.

I came home late on a wintry afternoon and was greeted by the welcome smell of food from the kitchen. "What's for dinner?" I called. My wife looked up from the stove. "Mr. Ehlers has been trying to reach you," she said. "You'd better call him before we eat."

I dialed genial Arthur. "Can you come down to the office at once?" he asked.

"I haven't had dinner . . ."

"This is important, Jimmie. Dinner can wait."

I broke speed laws on the way to Shibe Park and staggered into Arthur's office. "I know why you want to see me," I said. "I've heard rumors that the Old Man is thinking of hiring new coaches next season."

"You were never wronger, Jim. We're having lunch with him tomorrow at the Ben Franklin Hotel."

"Must I wait for tomorrow's lunch before I eat? Couldn't you have told me over the phone?"

"We're holding a press conference. You'll want to be prepared."

"For what?"

"Mr. Mack is announcing his retirement. He's picked you to manage the Athletics."

I was stricken speechless. During the last months of the season Mr. Mack had visibly aged. I had taken over some of his bench duties but I had assumed that Earl Mack would succeed him as manager when and if he retired. Now that moment had come and, of all the men in baseball, he had chosen me. I was overwhelmed.

I didn't think of the problems I would face. I only thought of the honor I was receiving, that of succeeding one of the founding fathers of the American League, Mr. Baseball himself in Philadelphia for fifty years.

I listened as Arthur recited the series of events which had led to Mr. Mack's withdrawal.

I had no appetite for dinner when I finally went home . . .

I sat beside Mr. Mack at the luncheon. I heard him say, "I am happy to announce that the Athletics will be in the capable hands of Jimmie Dykes next year."

Then I rose and told the writers what managing the Athletics meant to me.

In calmer moments I realized that I had an enormous job on my hands. The club was sinking into the quicksands of financial catastrophe. The team would be much the same as the tailenders of 1950: pitching weak, bench thin, no funds available for replacements. I'd have no difficulty in obtaining Arthur Ehlers' co-operation, but I was less than confident that Earl Mack's would be forthcoming.

In difficult situations a manager puts on a brave front. I kept smiling. I assured the newspapermen who accompanied the team south that I had a bunch of hustling go-getters. I even issued a statement that the Athletics were the most promising team I'd ever taken north. I seriously believed that, barring injuries, the '51 Athletics would rise in the standings high enough to stick a feather in my cap.

But when the season opened grim reality smacked me in the face. We lost thirteen straight before little Bobby Shantz brought us out of the tailspin with a well-pitched game. Then seven more defeats before Bobby won another. Throughout May Bobby was unbeatable. He continued to win until Al Rosen of the Indians set him down with a home run on June 24. By then he had won eleven of our twenty-two victories.

Meantime, I had obtained Gus Zernial from the White Sox. My old Hollywood slugger lifted the team out of its rut. Ferris Fain was almost always on base when Gus went to bat, and runs were no longer hard to get. Eddie Joost was ranging far and wide at short-stop. Harry Byrd, a strong young righthander, was clicking off wins. By August we had a fast, interesting team, sharp on defense, dangerous at bat. We won 29 of our last 41 games and included among our victims the strongest teams in the league. Only our miserable start prevented us from finishing higher than sixth.

I really felt that Philadelphia might play an important role in the American League race in 1952.

I was not far wrong. Fain, who had won the batting title in '51, repeated with a .327 average. Zernial, '51's home-run champion, continued to splash power. Our defenses were settled. Bobby Shantz was sensational, winning 24 games. He was supported by Harry Byrd, who took 15. A slow start again held us back, but I was satisfied with our fourth-place finish. I thought we were on our way to better things. Don't blame me for hoping that we might soon be strong enough to challenge the ever-winning Yankees.

I am the optimistic type, perhaps overoptimistic at times. I could see the proof of our progress in the league standings, but I disregarded our weakness at the gate. Only 627,100 fans passed through the turnstiles at Shibe Park in 1952. Philadelphia had become indifferent to the Athletics. Long years in the second division were taking their toll. Stories were published that winter that the franchise might be sold and transferred to another city. A committee of local businessmen was formed in an effort to keep the team in the city it had represented since 1901.

To add to my increasing gloom came the news that

Mr. Mack was failing. He had attended every game at home or abroad during the previous season but now he seldom appeared at his office in the ball park. One day before spring training began I went to Roy Mack's home to confer with Mr. Mack. He lay in bed. For an hour and a half I discussed the team. I say discussed the team for he was showing obvious signs of his advanced age. His mind often wandered. He was ninety-one years old.

I bade him good night. It should have been good-bye. I never saw him again in life.

The 1953 season began as all seasons begin, with high hopes. By May my hopes were shattered. Bobby Shantz tore a muscle in his pitching arm, which had been injured the previous September. The little fellow had carried us into the first division in '52 with his clever pitching and superb fielding. Now he was all but lost, starting but one more game the rest of the season.

Then our infield wall, the defensive key behind our pitchers, crumbled; Eddie Joost, vital at shortstop, sprained his knee while sliding and went on the injured list.

Next our outfield was ripped apart. Elmer Valo, the right fielder who dove into the stands to grab would-be home runs and whose arm was the equal of any in the league, tore a muscle in his leg and was reduced to pinch-hitting chores.

And Ferris Fain, our hit-and-run man, fell far off form, batting only .256.

We had no money to plug holes, no bench strength. We reeled through the season into seventh place.

Only 362,684 Philadelphians paid their way into Shibe Park.

I was delivering a talk about baseball in a Norristown club one November evening. As the applause died down a Philadelphia reporter plucked my sleeve. "I saw an Associated Press bulletin in my office before I came up here," he said. "It says that Eddie Joost is to manage the Athletics next year."

I was neither surprised nor shocked. "If the AP says so it must be true," I said.

I had bitter thoughts later that night. Managing a ball club is the world's chanciest job. Exchanging one manager for another is the cheapest way to inject new interest into a losing club. I should have known that my number was up. The press had been hinting that a shake-up in the Athletics' top echelon was due. Arthur Ehlers had already resigned to become general manager of the Baltimore Orioles, formerly the St. Louis Browns. As in Philadelphia, St. Louis had turned thumbs down on a perpetual loser. Would the A's take heels to another city soon? If so, it would not be my concern.

I consoled myself by the fact that I was in good company. The Indians had fired Lou Boudreau in 1950, two years after he'd won a flag for Cleveland and Bill Veeck. Charlie Dressen had been ousted by the Dodgers a few days after losing the 1953 World Series to the Yanks.

But I was angry because Earl Mack, who now sat in his father's executive chair, had not done me the courtesy of telling me that I was through before releasing the news of Eddie Joost's hiring to the press.

OUT OF THE FRYING PAN . . .

I WAS NOT idle long. As soon as Arthur Ehlers learned that I was at liberty, he contacted me. Within one week I had signed a contract to manage the Baltimore Orioles.

I found Baltimore in a frenzy of enthusiasm at the prospect of rooting for a big-league team. I was somewhat less enthusiastic. The Orioles were the same Browns who had been boycotted the previous season in St. Louis after losing twenty straight games at home, a league record. The only difference was that the Browns had been on the verge of bankruptcy in St. Louis, whereas the Orioles were rolling in the money of thirteen Maryland millionaire backers who'd banded together to bring big-time ball to the town of crab cakes and Chesapeake Bay oysters.

I had no illusions about the Orioles. As the Browns they'd been last in batting, last in fielding, and last in the American League standings, five games worse than my Athletics, 45½ games below the five-time pennant winners, those damn Yankees.

I met my new charges in training camp. They looked like ballplayers, they acted like ballplayers. But were they big-league ballplayers?

Vern Stephens had been in the majors since 1941; he'd been a good hitter, an established infielder, but he was thirty-four years old. Clint Courtney was an aggressive catcher. In the outfield were Vic Wertz, a veteran long-ball hitter, and Sam Mele, a smart flycatcher. My eye was caught by three hard-throwing young pitchers, Bob Turley, Don Larsen and Ryne Duren.

I adopted a policy of wait and see.

On opening day I saw little to startle me except the bands, the banners, and the capacity crowd. We won our first game. The fans celebrated as if we'd won a pennant.

I knew that the owners were willing to spend any amount for players. An opportunity arose when Earl Mack proposed a deal for my old Hollywood No. 4 man, Gus Zernial, who was still banging out home runs for the Athletics, 42 of them the previous year. Arthur Ehlers and Earl were conducting negotiations. Arthur informed me that Zernial and Dave Philley had nearly come to blows with Eddie Joost in an argument on the bench and that Earl had proposed a package deal consisting of Zernial for Wertz, first baseman Dick Kry-

howski, three lesser players—and $100,000. "I'm veto-
ing the deal," I told Arthur. "Gus is past his peak. He
won't hit nearly as many homers in our big park as in
Philadelphia. It's not worth that bundle of dough."

The next day I was in Arthur's office when Earl
phoned from Philadelphia. Arthur gestured that I
should pick up an extension phone.

"Are you ready to conclude the Zernial deal?" I
heard Earl ask.

"On the same basis as in our last conversation?"

"I might make some changes." Earl rattled off the
names of several players other than Wertz, Kryhowski
and the three throw-ins.

"How about the cash?"

"I must insist on one hundred grand."

I shook my head vigorously. Earl was determined to
put a big chunk of Oriole money in the Athletics' bank
account. "Jimmie Dykes won't go for this kind of a
deal," said Arthur.

Bargaining began. Earl stood firm, conceded, rallied,
retreated. Finally he came down to a flat $35,000. I was
dizzy from shaking my head. "I can't agree unless Jimmie approves," Arthur concluded.

I heard Earl's deep sigh. "Wish Jimmie was on our
side now. He was a good manager for us."

The deal was dead.

Bob Turley fanned thirteen Tigers, walked as many,
yet somehow wasn't scored on. "You were wonderfully
patient, Jimmie," said coach Tom Oliver after the game.
"I'd have given him the hook early and late."

"How can you take a pitcher out who only gives two
hits?" I asked.

"Lucky Dykes!" said Tiger manager Freddie Hutchinson the next day. "Thirteen walks and not a run . . . you've got a leprechaun on your shoulder."

Turley could blaze the ball, but seldom knew where it was going. He led the league in walks that year with 181 and in strikeouts with 185. It was a harrowing experience for a manager. I let him stay in to win 14 games while losing 15.

Our clutch hitting was nil. I had a standing bet of a nickel with my coaches that any runner who reached third base would not score. I was something like $27.55 ahead by All-Star Game time.

Don Larsen was our triple-threat man. He could pitch, hit, and stay out all night. Ryne Duren could throw harder and wilder than any pitcher I have ever seen. If he ever gained control he would be a right-handed Mose Grove.

These were my highest-flying Orioles. It would take time and trades with the Yankees to put their feet on the ground.

Among my pitchers in this curious season was Bobo Newsome, age forty-two. I tried out Bobo's well-worn arm in an exhibition game with the Phillies. He was leading, 6 to 1, in the sixth inning, when Bing Miller, again my coach, said, "Bobo will collapse if you don't take him out soon."

"You've had it for today," I told Newsome when he came in from the mound. "Go sit down somewhere."

He looked outraged. "What? Taking me out when I'm five runs ahead?"

I turned my back and went to the water cooler. I felt a hot breath on my neck and two powerful arms clasped me. "Them was the sweetest words I ever did hear, bo," Bobo purred in my ear. He released me and collapsed onto a corner of the bench. It was Newsome's last big-league show. At his own request I released the game old pitcher a few days later.

Our RBI figures were appallingly low. I called a meeting and drew a diagram of a diamond on the blackboard. "This is first base. Here's second and this is third. The object of the game of baseball is to touch all bases and then touch home plate, scoring a run. The team with the most runs wins the game. How many of you know this?"

No one said a word. No one smiled at my sarcasm. They continued to act as if the ground under home plate was mined with a high explosive that would explode if they planted their feet on it.

In a game with the Boston Red Sox we inexplicably scored seven runs in one inning. Suddenly I felt a sharp pain in my left side. I closed my eyes and breathed deeply. The pain grew worse. I was so frightened that I murmured a prayer: "Dear God, if I've got to go, take me now when we're seven runs ahead."

God saw fit to spare me. The pain was gone by the ninth inning when Boston tied the score. The Almighty rewarded me by making the Red Sox shortstop fumble in the tenth. We won but I was exhausted.

Before the June 15 cut-down date we obtained Cal Abrams from the Pirates. Pirate Manager Fred Haney sent me a wire:

NOW THAT YOU'VE GOT ABRAMS WHAT ARE YOU GOING TO DO WITH HIM?

Haney's wire was an implied reminder that Cal was a "clubhouse lawyer." I would have put nine clubhouse lawyers into the lineup if they knew how to win. I used Cal as the Orioles' regular right fielder. He led the team at bat with a .293 average. He became so popular that Baltimore fans, hungry for heroes, organized a

Day for him. He helped them by calling on merchants to inform them what he had done for dear old Baltimore and collected enough loot to furnish the Taj Mahal.

Among the close observers of the Oriole doings was Clarence Miles, the richest of the thirteen millionaires and therefore president of the club. Before the season began, Mr. Miles admitted that he knew nothing about baseball. By August he had mastered techniques and procedures and was freely telling me that I should have bunted for a sacrifice instead of going for a hit-and-run and otherwise second-guessing my tactics. After all, he was club president and I had to listen respectfully to his outpourings.

Before a night game he called me on the carpet for letting a pitcher remain in the box in the previous day's game. I accepted the responsibility and added that I would stand back of any decision I made. Our conversation was becoming quite crisp when I noticed that it was ten minutes to eight. "I have to take the line-up to the umpires in about five minutes," I said, and rose.

"Just a minute, Dykes," called Mr. Miles as I headed for the door. "Wipe that grass off the seat of your pants before you go on field."

"That isn't grass, Mr. Miles. For your information, it's mistletoe."

The Orioles lost 100 games. They didn't finish last. The Athletics lost 103.

I'd had enough. I resigned. I also vowed that never again would I manage. My experience with the Orioles had been the most trying of my career. I had yielded to my habit of believing that I could rally any team from the depths. The Orioles' owners were amateurs in a business which was rapidly becoming more and more complex. Early in the season they'd become dissatisfied with my cool professionalism. The team was impossibly weak. I'd been forced to suffer with it until the term of my contract expired.

Despite bad baseball the season had been a financial success. Attendance was 1,060,910, fourth in the league. The owners had set a goal of 1,500,000. When they realized that they would fall short of that figure someone suggested that the bleacher turnstile be whirled at the rate of 7,500 a game for the remainder of the season at the cost of 25 cents per whirl paid to visiting clubs. Arthur Ehlers had vetoed this absurd attempt to pad attendance figures.

7

BYE, BYE, BIRDIE

I was out of the big leagues but not out of baseball. I accepted an offer to teach the game at a clinic for our overseas forces at the air base in Weisbaden, Germany. The facilities for baseball, football, basketball and boxing were superb. The enthusiasm of the young men who participated was highly stimulating to an old-timer like me. After two months in the early summer of 1955 I became so delighted with the program that I volunteered to remain for two more years. Unfortunately the commanding officer at the base was not authorized to sign sports consultants and I reluctantly returned home.

Apparently my career was over. At last I was free to

play golf, smoke as many of my favorite cigars as I pleased, talk over old times with my cronies and take it easy for the rest of my days. An official of Philadelphia radio station WCAU convinced me that since I was an inveterate talker I might as well have an audience and talk before a mike for pay. I gladly accepted.

Fifteen minutes after I'd agreed to become a sports commentator the telephone, that persistent disrupter of my peace of mind, rang. My wife answered. A moment later she called, "It's Birdie Tebbetts on long distance."

That old firehorse in me trotted to the phone. Birdie and I had been good friends since my early White Sox days when he'd been the Tigers' star catcher and I'd tried to get him in a deal. He was a great guy.

Now he was managing Cincinnati. His first words were, "Jim, I'm short a coach. How about coming out of hiding and joining me?"

Well, Dykes, why not? What were the comforts of home compared to constant travel, hotel beds, and restaurant food? What was taking it easy compared to making the baseball rounds?

"Where are the Reds playing?"

"In Cincinnati."

"I'll be there on the next plane."

I was back in baseball and in the National League for the first time. Birdie and I got along famously. I was his third-base coach, taking his signs and relaying them to batters and base runners. The Reds were a hard-hitting team, bristling with the bats of Ted Kluszewski, Frank Robinson, Wally Post, Gus Bell, and Smoky Burgess. Their general manager was young and aggressive Gabe Paul.

The National League impressed me as superior to

the American, faster, better balanced. I credited this to the Negro players who'd been signed in the years after Jackie Robinson had broken the color line with the Dodgers in 1947, whereas American League clubs had lagged in this respect. The all-around play of Willie Mays, Henry Aaron, Ernie Banks, and other Negroes was exciting to watch. They reminded me of the superstars of my playing days.

I'd been a manager for years; Birdie was relatively new to the trade. In an early chat I said, "Never tell me what you think about a player while we're in the dugout, even if you whisper it in my ear while we're sitting side by side on the bench. If there's a doubt about some decision you've made, talk to me about it after the game. I'm no yes-man. I'll give you my honest opinion. I'll tell you the truth."

The Reds were a happy club. Birdie worked intelligently with his pitchers. "Remember, you're the biggest man on the field," he'd tell them. "Every play starts with your delivering the ball. Let batters know that you're their enemy. You've got the ball. They've got to hit it. Stay on top. Think of yourself as the best and show it." To relief pitchers he said, "When you're called into a game, think of it as a challenge. Don't come from the bullpen head down. Keep it up, even when the bases are full. Take charge! Be the coolest man on the field. Use your head! Outthink 'em." Then a pat on the fanny and he had a man with a strong winning spirit.

Birdie studied each player as an individual. He knew their backgrounds, their psychological patterns and their ballplaying potentialities. His easy affability contributed to the harmony on the club.

He could even read my mind.

During a night game in Pittsburgh I wore special

lenses to help me pick up Birdie's signs from the bench.
Two were out, a runner on third and two strikes on
the batter, Johnny Temple. I glanced at Birdie. To my
astonishment he was wiggling two fingers in the
squeeze sign. I looked again. He was still wiggling two
fingers.

I knew Birdie would never order a squeeze bunt in
such a situation. If the bunt went foul or Temple missed
the ball the side would be retired.

To get a better view I went to the end of the coaching box and squinted. Birdie was still wiggling.

Suddenly he bellowed: "Hey, ya meathead!"

Reluctantly I gave the sign. Temple couldn't believe
his eyes. The Pirate pitcher threw a high fast ball.
Temple popped a foul. He was out on a technical third
strike.

I hustled to the dugout to get the first word in:
"Look here, Birdie, what's the idea of a squeeze?"

"I'm the meathead," he admitted. "I thought the
scoreboard said one was out instead of two."

I pulled off my glasses. "You need these special
lenses worse than I do," I laughed.

The same two-out, runner-on-third situation came up
at Ebbets Field not long afterwards. At bat was our
shortstop, Roy McMillan, an expert bunter. I squinted
into our dugout. Birdie was giving the finger wiggle for
another squeeze bunt.

"No, no, no!" I shouted, throwing up my hands.

Birdie laughed, then gave me his hit sign. McMillan
slashed one through the box and the runner scored.

"I was giving you the meathead test," chuckled
Birdie as I came in. "If you ever let me pull a boner
like that Pittsburgh mess you can go hunt a new job."

I had many a good laugh with Birdie until the 1958 season got under way. The Reds had finished third in '56 and fourth in '57. We had the power but not the pitching. Expectations were high as '58 began, for Gabe Paul was bringing promising youngsters up from the farms.

Cincinnati lives and dies with its ball club. The season was a sad disappointment. The Reds dawdled through July deep in the second division. Sportswriters panned Birdie. Fans booed him whenever he stuck his nose out of the dugout. His strategy was criticized, his tactics were pulled apart, and some didn't like the way he combed his hair. I suspected that something was in the air when Gabe Paul notified us three coaches, Johnny Riddle, Tom Ferrick and me, that we would not be rehired in 1959.

One August evening after we had dropped 12 out of 16 games, Birdie told me that he'd had enough. More than pride was involved; his professional integrity was under attack. He had decided to resign. He'd discussed his decision with his wife, Mary, and she'd agreed that he should quit.

For hours after the game I argued that he wasn't to blame for the team's fall into last place. The players were in a general slump because they were trying too hard to win. As a result batters were failing in the clutch and pitchers were laboring. It was a difficult theory to prove. I did my best but Birdie said, "I'd rather quit now than be fired later."

I realized that his decision was unshakable.

The next morning I was breakfasting at the Netherlands-Plaza Hotel with umpire Al Barlick when a page called me to the phone. "Come to my office before you go to the ball park," said Gabe Paul.

When I arrived at his office Gabe informed me that Birdie had formally resigned. "I'd appreciate your taking over the club temporarily," he added.

"How long is temporary?"

"Three or four days."

"Will do."

At Crosley Field Birdie was packing his personal belongings.

"Have you any idea who's to be the new manager?" I asked.

With a curious smile that made me suspect he was not telling the truth he said, "I have no idea."

Within minutes I'd pried from him the information that Mayo Smith, then managing the Phillies, was Gabe Paul's choice.

That Thursday afternoon I directed the Reds to victory over the league-leading Milwaukee Braves. We lost to the Braves the following evening. Then we won a day game on Saturday afternoon. After the game Gabe phoned me, asking me to bring the other coaches over to his office on Sunday morning.

Before his office door Riddle, Ferrick and I shook hands on a pledge to tell Mr. Paul to shove his team on a slow boat to Zanzibar if he so much as dared criticize us. We expected to be fired. The choice of coaches is a manager's prerogative, and Mayo Smith had the right to get rid of us for his own aides if, as I believed, he was taking over the Reds.

To our surprise, Gabe was all milk and honey. Would I agree to manage the Reds for the remaining seven weeks of the season?

How could I say No?

On my way to the ball park I bought a copy of the Cincinnati *Enquirer*. Black headlines on the sports page proclaimed that Mayo Smith would manage the Reds in 1959. The writer was Bill Ford. The source of the story was me. In the course of a chat with Ford on Saturday I'd mentioned Smith as winner in the Reds' managerial derby. I had neglected to tell Ford that I was speaking off the record. His story made me feel as if I had breached a confidence.

Ford was already at Crosley Field when I arrived. "You've put me on a big black spot," he said. "I hope that story stands up."

"It's the truth," I said. "Smith would probably be here today if the Reds weren't in last place."

I made a quick decision. I called the team together behind the closed doors of the clubhouse. "I'm your interim manager for the rest of the season," I announced. "Whether you play your heads off or continue as you've been doing makes no personal difference to me. No matter what happens I'm out. But my advice is play your best or you won't be able to ask for a raise when contract-signing time comes around. I shan't call another meeting this season. Frankly, I don't care what you do. It's up to you. Any questions?"

There were none.

We beat the Braves that afternoon. That night we flew to the Pacific Coast. We knocked off the San Francisco Giants three straight. In Los Angeles we cut down the Dodgers to size. Suddenly we were the hottest team in the league. Batters came through with timely blows. Our pitchers bore down. Pitchers tightened control, bore down, stopped rallies. By mid-September we were rising rapidly in the close National League race. We finished fourth. Since August 14, when I had taken over the team, we had won 24 games, lost 17.

I do not know why the Reds suddenly took fire after that clubhouse meeting. Perhaps they had been trying too hard to win for Birdie, whom they warmly admired. I had made no changes in the lineup. I merely sent them on the field, that's all. They had played snappy, heads-up ball. They'd done it all by themselves.

Others didn't think so. Two prominent sports columnists, Lou Smith of the *Enquirer* and Johnny Carmichael of the Chicago *Daily News*, started campaigns in late September to nominate me as the Reds' manager in 1959. They got a rise out of Gabe Paul, who had not yet officially announced Mayo Smith's hiring. Gabe retorted that he wanted a young, active man, which led Smith and Carmichael to point out that that year's pennant-winning managers, Casey Stengel of the Yankees and Fred Haney of the Braves, were as much in their sixties as I was, Casey sixty-seven, Fred sixty, whereas I was sixty-two.

I found myself in the midst of a controversy which I had not invited. The Associated Press asked me to comment on the implication that I was too old to manage. "I'm as physically and mentally able to lead a team as I was twenty-five years ago in Chicago," I said. "Mr. Paul has made no commitment to me. He has the right to sign anybody he pleases."

This was true, of course. I had no kick. Gabe had not offered me a bonus for acting as interim manager, but he had given me a check at the end of the season which had almost doubled my salary as coach.

Now he made Mayo Smith's hiring official.

I was out of a job, as far too many qualified managers are.

TIGER, TIGER, BURNING BRIGHT

BUT NOT FOR LONG. I went to Milwaukee for the World Series opener. Danny Murtaugh grabbed me by the arm. "I can use you as a coach next season, Jim, if you're usable."

"I'm as usable as ever," I said, cuffing Danny on the chin.

"Boy, you're on the team!"

I reported to the Pirates' camp in Fort Myers, Florida, the following March. I felt like a frisky colt let out of the barn. Danny was the cheerful up-and-coming manager of a team which had finished second the previous year. And Fort Myers was where I had trained with the Athletics thirty years earlier when Mr. Mack was trimming 'em down for their great pennant drive of 1929. The '59 Pirates reminded me of my old team. They were young, ambitious, on the upbeat. Danny was an old friend. Joe E. Brown was a young, enthusiastic general manager. It promised to be a happy year.

The Pirates outlasted the Cardinals in a hard-fought game one day early in May. They were noisily celebrating their victory in the clubhouse when the phone in Danny's office rang. "It's for you, Jim," he said. "Rick Ferrell's calling from Detroit."

Rick Ferrell had graduated from long and distinguished service as a star American League catcher into the general managership of the Detroit Tigers. He was a sunny, good-natured guy with many friends and no enemies.

What on earth did he want with me?

He came straight to the point: "Bill Norman is out as Tiger manager," he said. "Jim, the job's yours if you want it."

I did a quick double-think. I was enjoying life with the Pirates. The Tigers had begun the season in a long slump and were in last place. I'd vowed never again to manage a loser after my sad experience with the Orioles. I was more than a little weary of dragging tail-enders out of the mire and getting muddied in the process. "Thanks, Rick," I stalled, "but I'll have to take this up with Joey Brown."

"Let me talk to Joe," said Rick.

I had the call transferred to Brown's office. A few minutes later he burst into the clubhouse. "Congratulations, Jimmie!" he cried. "You're the new manager of the Tigers!"

"I'm not sure I want to leave Pittsburgh."

"You can always come back. There are only two jobs you can't have here, Danny's and mine."

Danny put in the clincher: "Remember what I told you when I took this job. Where else could I make the kind of money managers get?"

"Okay . . . I'll go."

Rick was waiting. We talked terms. I agreed to fly to Detroit that night.

When I broke the news to my wife she exclaimed: "What? Again? I thought you swore never to put your neck in a noose again."

"Forgive me, Mary. I guess managing is in my blood."

I took off for Detroit in a gully-jumping plane that landed in Youngstown to catch its breath. There I bought a newspaper which, to my dismay, told me that the Tigers were scheduled to meet the damn Yankees in a doubleheader the next day, a Sunday. I hoped the plane would tumble into Lake Erie on the way to Detroit.

I checked over the Tigers' roster in my mind. They certainly didn't look like a team which should be wallowing in last place. They had two consistent .300 hitters in Al Kaline and Harvey Kuenn. And three dependable starters: Jim Bunning, Frank Lary and Don Mossi. After landing I learned more from Rick and Jim Campbell, the club's vice-president, who met me at the airport. The following morning the coaches, who included Billy Hitchcock, my Athletic third sacker in 1950, said that player morale was abysmally low after losing 15 of the first 17 games.

I glanced through recent box scores. "Why hasn't Charlie Maxwell been used?" I inquired. The coaches didn't know. Maxwell had caught my eye in my last year in the American League. He was a good outfielder who could drive an occasional long ball. "Let's put him in left field today and see how he looks," I suggested.

Then I girded myself for coming battles with Detroit baseball writers and with the unsinkable Yankees.

I shall never forget that Sunday doubleheader. I thought I was a lucky stiff when Maxwell rifled a line-drive home run to right in his first time up in the first game. I looked for horseshoes in the dugout when he followed it with a longer homer later in the game. We won.

I considered myself a magician when Maxwell slammed No. 3 in the nightcap. I was nothing less than a genius when he walloped No. 4, a game-winner.

Monday's papers called Charlie the juice the Tigers needed to get started. They called me a miracle worker for beating the unbeatable Yankees in two games. In my own book I was just a lucky stiff.

Beating the bombed-out Bombers twice in one day pulled team morale out of the abyss. Kaline and Kuenn began to do what comes naturally to intelligent hitters. Eddie Yost, the veteran third sacker, not only collected his usual quota of walks but he also found the home-run range. The three starters reeled off complete games. Suddenly the Tigers were the sensation of the league. They won 32 of the 45 games between my arrival and mid-June. They climbed from the basement to the airy heights of second place. Can you blame me for dreaming of a pennant?

It was not to be. Kaline, our cleanup hitter and far-flying right fielder, suffered a broken jaw and, although he missed only a few games, he fell below par for the rest of the season. Other injuries slowed us down. We finished no better than fourth, but fourth was only the Tigers' second first-division berth in nine seasons.

The season was a success. I was a success to fans who remembered how the team had responded to my leadership at the time of its sensational spurt. I had had little to do with the spurt. I'd merely used my usual methods of keeping a ball club on its toes by relaxing the boys from tension. A manager is at the mercy of his players. I'd merely tried to keep mine carefree and loose. The rest is in the books, calling the right plays, using the best men available, settling the rotation of pitchers. To me, this was routine.

I was in an optimistic mood as I took my annual jaunt to the World Series, Rick Ferrell my companion. The White Sox had finally put together the pieces and were about to battle the Dodgers in the big-money games. On the evening before the opening game Rick and I were socializing with newspapermen in the Chicago press headquarters when a loudspeaker suddenly foreshadowed doom. Over the buzzing of conversation and the clicking of typewriters came the announcement:

"William O. DeWitt has been named president of the Detroit Tigers."

I swallowed hard. "We'd better slip over to Detroit, Rick," I said, "and sign my contract for next year before Bill DeWitt throws a monkey wrench into the works. I don't think he likes me much."

"Easy does it, Jim," said Rick. "I'll stand by my

agreement with you to manage the Tigers next year and as long as you want to stay. I give you my solemn word on that."

Bill DeWitt was a baseball career man, a protégé of Branch Rickey's. I first came into contact with him in 1939 when I was managing the White Sox and he was general manager of the St. Louis Browns. I had offered to trade Rip Radcliff, a good-hitting first baseman and outfielder, to the Browns during the winter meetings. News became scarce while the deal hung fire. A St. Louis reporter with a blank sheet of paper in his typewriter wrote a story that I was trying to foist a palooka on helpless Mr. DeWitt.

DeWitt didn't read the story until after the deal was completed. He accused me of planting it in advance to cover myself in case the deal blew up in his face.

I burned. "You'd better put someone in your office who can tell a palooka from a big-league ball player," I said.

He walked away in a huff.

It was a trifling incident and I forgot it. The following season the White Sox visited St. Louis. DeWitt invaded our dugout and made loud remarks reflecting on my integrity. I told him he had no business in our private bailiwick, adding a few choice comments of my own as I led him by the arm out of the dugout. Since then I'd had no dealings with him.

I had a premonition that my happy days with the Tigers would soon be over.

My fears were realized as soon as the Tigers' camp got under way in Lakeland, Florida, in March 1960.

Until then I had received authority from every club executive to agree to the disposition of players on the roster. Now DeWitt presumed to tell me which Tigers should be retained, which sent down, and, on one occasion, whom I should play in the opening-day lineup. I avoided arguing with him. I avoided talking to him as much as possible. I had no desire for a showdown. Live and let live had been my maxim from the first day I'd worn a baseball uniform in Gettysburg forty-odd years earlier. But I was wary, on guard.

Farm clubs were in training at Tigertown, half a mile from the Big Team's base. I sent for some minor-league pitchers to throw batting practice to our Tiger hitters in order to give them an early start on getting into form. Charlie Metro, manager of the AAA Denver farm team, objected. It was a minor matter that could have been settled over cigars and a couple of bottles of beer.

But when Metro arrived at our base DeWitt joined us and turned what might have been a friendly give-and-take into a formal meeting, with himself in the chair.

From the start I realized that DeWitt was intent on deciding the issue in Metro's favor.

"Mr. DeWitt," I interrupted, "why don't you stop putting your two cents' worth in? You know nothing about this problem. Are you more interested in Denver than in the Tigers? I'd like a frank answer, please."

He glared. "Naturally I'm interested in both clubs."

"Well, whether you like it or not I'm going to use two or three of Charlie Metro's pitchers to help our hitters round into form. I don't want a repetition of last season's April slump. I'm going to do everything I can to get the Big Team off to a fine start."

I won my point, but I failed to convince DeWitt that
a manager must make use of every one of his organization's resources if he is to put his team into contention.
The Tigers got off to a good start, winning five straight,
then slumped. DeWitt offered me free advice every
day. Within weeks he'd stuck his finger into every piece
of Tiger pie. He was at odds with Doc Fenkel, the club
secretary, for admitting two visiting celebrities into his
private box. He was at war with the custodian of the
parking lot for insisting on knowing the names of the
owners of every car in the lot. He told the grounds
keeper how to cut the grass and ordered him to land-
scape the grounds of the house he had bought in the
city.

But what irked me most was that no detail of Tiger
play was too small for his eagle eye. He was not satisfied with watching home games in the flesh and road
games on TV. He sent Rick Ferrell on the road with us,
ordering him to report over the telephone after each
game about every happening on the field, in the dugout and the clubhouse. He was Big Brother, listening
in, watching through walls; he was everywhere.

A clash was due and it came. DeWitt proposed to
trade Harvey Kuenn to Cleveland for Rocky Colavito.
Kuenn had won the 1959 batting title with a splendid
.353. He averaged 200 hits per season and drew from
65 to 75 walks. He was on base at least once in every
game. Harvey's swing was classic, even, smart, sure.
Rocky was a home-run threat every time at bat—he'd
hit 42 homers in '59—but he'd hit only .257, almost
100 points under Harvey. I protested that Harvey was
the superior offensive player, a hitter who controlled
his bat, a team man, not an individualist.

I thought I'd won the argument until Rick Ferrell

came to the dugout before a game. "You may as well take Kuenn out of today's lineup," he told me. "DeWitt traded him to the Indians this morning."

When Kuenn came in from practice I told him that he was no longer a Tiger. "I want you to know that I've had nothing to do with the deal," I said.

The deal shocked Cleveland fans, to whom Rocky was a hero. It shocked Rocky, too. Conscientious player that he is, he couldn't get going with us. The result was precisely as I had foreseen. We swapped consistency for the occasional long blast.

I kept Kaline in the lineup although he was hitting below par, because I felt that a batter with his natural ability could work himself out of a slump. DeWitt wanted me to bench him and put Sandy Amoros in his place. He had obtained Amoros from the Dodgers and asserted that Buzzy Bavasi had assured him that the little Cuban was still at the peak of his game. "Sandy's over the hill," I said. "Bavasi wouldn't send a good player to his mother if she was managing any other big-league club than the Dodgers."

I settled by giving Kaline a six-day rest. Amoros made one hit in those six games. "You're playing every day from now on," I told Al. "Go out and do what comes natural to you."

He did—and he's still doing it.

One Sunday we lost two tense games, 1 to 0 and 2 to 1. After the double defeat DeWitt descended on me at my locker, violating the rule that general managers must not enter the clubhouse while players are present. He told me to bench Eddie Yost. I happened to know that Eddie was leading the league in wheedling walks, and had been on base 58 per cent of the time. I argued that I had no other comparable lead-off man. "What good is getting on, when he doesn't score?" DeWitt said. "And that goes for Fernandez, too. He can't hit his weight!"

He was gone before I could answer his criticism. I noticed that a newspaperman in the clubhouse had overheard part of our conversation. I decided to speak out before DeWitt made matters worse by criticizing Yost and Fernandez to the press, so I asked the newsman to round up his colleagues for a brief conference.

When the others arrived I told them that I was assuming full responsibility for our double defeat. No, there'd be no changes in the lineup. Yes, I'd keep Chico Fernandez at short. "We got Chico from the Phillies to plug the gap at shortstop. That's what he's been doing. If you read today's statistical sheet you'll find he happens to lead the team in hitting this month. Now, if you have no more questions, I'm through. If I have anything else to say it will be after I have read the complete remarks of the Tiger president and know what's on his mind."

They laughed. One said that DeWitt hadn't made any remarks yet.

"Not even that he was in this clubhouse just now, where he had no business being?"

The feud was in the open. The tension between us mounted as DeWitt told me that he had bought Clem Labine from the Dodgers for $25,000. "Labine was worth a lot more in his day but his day is over," I said.

I used Labine in relief. He was hit hard. On a day when our starters were used up I let him start. He was knocked out in an early inning.

After the game came the usual phone call. "Why did you start Labine today?" asked DeWitt.

"He's on the staff, isn't he? You put him there yourself. I told you I didn't want him. You went ahead and
made the deal. He's another gift from Bavasi, who'll
never let a player go who'll haunt him later."

"I don't want you to start him any more!"

"If I run short of pitchers again I will."

Which I did, for I knew that unless DeWitt went
first I'd be through soon with the Tigers or surely after
the season ended.

On the plane to Pittsburgh for the All-Star Game I
mentioned my troubles to John E. Fetzler, who owned
a controlling interest in the Tigers. My warning was of
no avail. It was I who was to go, and most unexpectedly.

I was in New York, dining in the Stadium Club after
the loss of a fourteen-inning thriller to the Yankees
when Doc Fenkel, acting as our road secretary, appeared. "Rick Ferrell's waiting to see you in an office
downstairs," he said.

Rick's first words were: "Lost a tough one today,
huh?"

"I'm glad you were here to see it."

"I didn't see it. Just flew in on club business. Bill
DeWitt wants me to ask you if you are willing to swap
jobs with Joe Gordon."

"Say that again, Rick."

"Will you manage the Indians if Gordon comes to
Detroit to manage the Tigers?"

"Let's hear it once more."

"A trade, you numbskull! A trade of managers. You
go to Cleveland, Gordon comes to Detroit."

"Oh. . . . " When I got my breath my first thought
was to tell Bill DeWitt to go jump into Lake Michigan.

My second was to wonder if this was not one way out of the maze I was in. My third was to ask for Joe Gordon's reaction to the unprecedented deal.

"Joe's for it," said Rick. "How about you?"

"You're not kidding, pal, are you?"

"Frank Lane is in Washington with the Indians, waiting for your reply."

I was doing mental flipflops. After some clarification from Rick I landed on my feet. Two little words from me would rid me of Bill DeWitt for life.

I said them:

"I'll go."

Lane was an impulsive publicity-minded operator. He was apparently unhappy about Gordon's handling of the Indians, who had moved into first place in June only to skid into fourth place by July. I could imagine how DeWitt's proposal must have appealed to him as a means of putting the Indians on the nation's front pages if not back into first place in the American League.

DeWitt's motive was obvious. He'd had his fill of stubborn me.

Unlike players, managers cannot be traded without their consent. They sign contracts which they may cancel at any time. They also may be fired without notice provided they are paid the balance due them under their contracts.

The fact was that Gordon and I were doing a first. Never before had managers swapped jobs. Put an asterisk in the record books opposite our names, then forget about it.

Rick asked me whether I would remain overnight and manage the Tigers the next day. "Not me," I said. "I want no part of the Tigers, not now or in the future."

I flew to Detroit to close my personal affairs in that city. I called Frank Lane after I arrived. "I'm delighted," he said. "Gordon's on his way to join the Tigers. When can you arrive?"

I told Frank that I would take command of the Indians the following day.

The deed was done.

Should I have resigned when Rick told me about the "deal," and gone home to Philadelphia? What did I have to gain by assuming the burden of a new team in midseason? Deep inside I found the answer. Baseball was my way of life. Managing was my way of keeping alive the old spirit which had carried me through so many years of thrilling conflict. In Cleveland I could try again to teach younger men how to play the Jimmie Dykes brand of baseball.

I knew and liked Frank Lane. I'd be independent once more, unhampered by front office interference.

I had a taste of things to come when I visited Lane's office to sign my contract.

"Is there anything else you want, Jimmie?" he asked.

"Nothing more than my expenses for moving from Detroit to Cleveland."

He left the room. A few minutes later his secretary brought me a check. It was for $5,000.

For one week I closely observed my new charges. They were in fourth place after their nine-day stay on top in June. Harvey Kuenn was their most productive hitter, followed by John Francona, Vic Power and Jimmy Piersall. Pitching was sparse, with Jim Perry the sole reliable starter. The Indians were so-so, neither bad nor good.

Their general mood was one of indifference. The atmosphere on the bench and in the clubhouse was spiritless. I was shocked by the sloppy way batting practice was conducted. The schedule for pitchers, irregulars, and regulars was posted on the bulletin board, but several pitchers failed to show up and the others drifted on field whenever they pleased.

The third-base coach is responsible for keeping pre-game routines moving. He serves as the manager's good right arm. Jo-Jo White, who had been Gordon's aide, had followed him to Detroit. I arranged for the transfer to Cleveland of Luke Appling, who had served in this post at Detroit.

More than a switch in coaches was needed to wake up the club. "This team has been taking life too easy," I said at a clubhouse meeting. "Some of you have been coming out to batting practice late, others not at all. This must stop. From now on everyone reports at the batting cage at the time designated, pitchers and extra men as well as regulars. Loosen up before you take your cuts. Run the bases after you've swung. Everyone must observe the schedule.

"Put some pep into your fielding practice. Throw hard, don't lob. Give the early birds in the stands a show. Going through the motions is cheating yourself —and the fans. Put on a slick performance. Understand? Any questions?"

I'll say this for them—they understood and obeyed.

As a rule the manager does not concern himself with practice sessions unless a regular is slumping at bat. He may then go out and try to detect whether the player has fallen into bad hitting habits. If he believes the slumper needs a rest he may pull him out of the lineup for a rest. During my first season as White Sox

manager I had attended batting practices from start
to finish. Later I only watched the regulars hit, but as
time went on I seldom appeared on the field before
games except to fan the breeze with newspapermen.

In New York a journalist once caught me playing
solitaire, my favorite time waster, about half an hour
before a game.

"Why aren't you out watching your boys?" he asked.

"I've been managing for years and expect no overnight miracles," I chuckled. "I don't think any of my
boys are going to surprise me today."

I'd had no trouble with lazy players until I met the
Indians. I had none with them after that meeting.

On paper the Indians looked like a pretty good ball
club but they were obviously down in the mouth, list-
less, unsettled. I tried to find out what was responsible
for their lackadaisical play. It wasn't an internal squab-
ble or cliques in the club. There was, however, some
resentment against Jimmy Piersall, everybody's problem child. My first impression of Jimmy was not that
of a naughty boy or one beset with mental troubles.
My experiences with him in 1960 and 1961 convinced
me that Jimmy was a smart cookie who took advantage
of any opportunity to project himself into the public
eye.

His turns at bat were super productions. His antics
on base were comic turns. His posings in the field included bits of amusing pantomime. At the same time
he was hitting close to .300 and making dazzling
catches, a valuable player who belonged in the lineup
every day.

I watched him closely and noticed that he would

pick on umpires during the second games of Sunday doubleheaders and get himself tossed out.

I soon discovered the reason. Mondays were usually off-days in our schedule. If Jimmy could get himself ejected by 5 P.M. he had plenty of time to dress, taxi to the airport and catch an eight o'clock plane for Boston, where he would spend Sunday night, all day Monday and Monday night with his dearly beloved wife and children before rejoining the team for a Tuesday night game, whereas if he played the full doubleheader he would not be able to leave Cleveland before Monday morning.

I gave Jimmy an indirect warning that I was wise to his Sunday antics. I benched him in the first game of a twin bill. Between games he popped into my office. Before he could open his mouth I said: "The answer is Yes. You are playing the second game from start to finish! Get it?"

I also posted a notice that a player removed from a game for any reason might shower and dress for the street but must remain in the clubhouse until the game was over, the only exception being a starting pitcher who'd been knocked out of the box.

Jimmy got the message. Umpires spent the second games of Sunday doubleheaders in peace.

I had another problem child in Cleveland's second baseman, Johnny Temple, who'd been obtained from Cincinnati in one of Frank Lane's numerous deals. Johnny was in a highly nervous state; when I benched him he would blow sky high.

During a night game Johnny and Jimmy got into such a hot argument that I was afraid fisticuffs would break out. I stepped between the two battling boys. "The next man who opens his mouth will pay two

hundred bucks for it!" I decreed. "If you really want
blood we'll arrange a showdown bout after the game,
not on the bench in front of thousands of people. Now
shut up, the two of you!"

They did.

Before the '60 season ended I took Piersall aside for
a long fatherly talk. Among other pearls of advice I
gave him was: "You're a brilliant outfielder, but if you
prefer to be a comedian why not apply for a booking
at the Copacabana Club when we get to New York?
You will make more money clowning than in baseball.
Don't try out your comic stuff on me. I know nothing
about show business and never go to night clubs."

That afternoon Jimmy made one of his electrifying
one-hand catches, racing far back to grab the ball off
the fence.

Nate Wallack, our road secretary, showed me the list
of ticket requests by players for a series about to begin
in Boston. Opposite Jimmy's name were thirty-five requests, some for passes, some for paid seats. I foresaw
an elaborate comedy show from my extroverted center
fielder for the amusement of his friends and neighbors.
I summoned him. "You don't want to be disgraced by
being benched before the home folks, do you?"

He was a model of gentlemanly deportment throughout the series.

Piersall played fine ball for me, especially in 1961,
when he hit .322 and darted all over the outfield for
far-flung flies. Occasionally he would cut capers before
big crowds, but far oftener he was a dedicated star.

"You're the first manager with the guts to make
Piersall behave," Frank Lane told me. "He hasn't been
put out of a game for weeks."

I told him why. I had a secret agreement with

umpires not to oust Jimmy until I arrived on the scene, for he would calm down as soon as I laid a restraining hand on him. One day he argued a called strike with umpire Cal Drummond. I leaped from the bench but before I could intervene Drummond had banished him. It was his only ouster in months.

Early in '61 Jimmy was called out at second by umpire Johnny Stevens. He went into a wild dance, kicking dust on Stevens's shoes, and was given an immediate thumb.

"Why didn't you wait for me before putting Piersall out?" I asked Stevens the next day.

"He tried out some brand-new swear words on me."

Jimmy knew all the words, four-lettered and longer, and could make up a few of his own. He was a throwback to the days of rugged baseball, when players were personalities on the field.

I found his weak spot by accident. It was his pride.

Dick Stigman was pitching for us in New York. I heard a roar of laughter from the stands. A young fan had run into center field. Jimmy chased him and planted a kick in the seat of his pants.

It was an undignified way of getting rid of a pest who could have been removed by the police without adding a Keystone comedy touch to the incident. When the inning was over, I turned to Marty Keough, a reserve outfielder: "Go take Piersall's place. That clown is through for the day."

Jimmy confronted me, fire in his eye. "What's wrong with me?" he bawled. "I'm the best center fielder in the league, ain't I?"

"When you behave you are," I said.

He sat on the bench for the rest of the game. I swear I saw tears in his eyes.

In my wanderings around the big leagues I'd learned to accommodate myself to the crotchets of general managers, Bill DeWitt excepted. Frank Lane was easy to get along with. When he had something on his mind I had only to turn to the next day's paper to find out what it was, for he thought out loud to sportswriters. The Indians finished fourth in 1960, five games ahead of the sixth-place Tigers. Frank offered me a contract for '61 which I gladly accepted. I told him I thought I could move the team higher in '61, given a few improvements here and there. Cleveland was in dire need of a winner. Attendance had dropped from a high of approximately 2,600,000 in 1948 to 950,000 in 1960. Rumors were afloat that the franchise might be shifted to another city. This would have been a castastrophe to Vice-President Nate Dolin and other stockholders representing local interests.

In the meantime, Frank had concealed from me that his resignation was in the works. He soon transferred his activities to the Kansas City Athletics. Hoot Evers took his place on a temporary basis.

Despite this change in the front office the 1961 training season passed smoothly. The Indians were little changed from the previous year. After a month's play of the regular season we were at approximately the same level, in fifth place with a 12-13 record.

Suddenly everything clicked. Day after day we won, taking 22 of 26 games between May 13 and June 6. We flew into New York in the midst of a dizzy ten-game victory streak. I was preparing for bed around 2:30 A.M. when the phone rang.

"Nate Dolin's in town," said Nate Wallack. "He's with me now. Can you come up?"

"I'm in my pajamas ———"

"Hop into any old thing. He has someone with him who wants to see you."

That "someone" was Gabe Paul.

My onetime Cincinnati boss had quit the Reds to help organize the Houston Colt .45's, an expansion club. Earlier that week he had resigned. His presence in New York could only mean that he was about to become Frank Lane's successor as general manager.

For an hour we talked about the team and the expected effect of the winning streak on attendance in the next home stand. Not until I was snug in bed did I recall Gabe's last public utterance in the controversy about the Reds' managerial job in 1959, that he preferred a younger man than me.

That week the winning streak ended. On our return to Cleveland Gabe notified me that he wanted to meet the members of the team face to face. It was a revealing meeting. Gabe had apparently done his homework well. He talked about the necessity for economy and then announced some rules intended to bring it about.

Players would no longer be permitted to make personal calls or to conduct personal business in the clubhouse. Players would no longer be permitted to take their personal mail to the office for stamping and handling.

I could hardly object to these rules although from the economy point of view the amount of money saved would be picayune. But my back went up when he announced that he was banning the drinking of beer in the clubhouse after games. I am a firm believer in the value of beer as a mild stimulant which relaxes the tension that builds up in ballplayers during a hard game. Mr. Mack had permitted it and I had followed his practice wherever I had managed. Players who sip from a can or two of cold brew do not rush to a nearby saloon later to guzzle hard liquor. They do not sit around at tables where everyone buys a social drink, where arguments start and brawls erupt as they did in pre-Prohibition days.

Gabe had banned beer in Cincinnati. I had connived with a friendly attendant to hide a bottle or two of suds in a cool pail of water in the dungeonlike room where road uniforms were stored.

After the meeting I told Gabe he had the right to issue any order he pleased, but I objected to his ban on beer. I won my point. The Indians kept their beer.

I don't say that the slump which followed and which included seven straight defeats was due to Gabe's talk. He certainly did nothing to improve club morale. Among his remarks was a statement which implied the team was not playing its best. This came as a shock to players who were then three games ahead of their pace for the preceding month. I could tell from the expression on many faces that the boys had expected praise from their new boss, not implied criticism and the withdrawal of minor but visible privileges.

The cold truth about the Indians was that they were not strong enough to win the pennant. Maris and Mantle, Ford and Berra were off on a furious drive to bring one more flag to the damn Yankees. Before the season started I had handed my prediction of the final standings in a sealed envelope to Regis McCauley, the Cleveland sportswriter, in which I awarded the Indians fourth place. I was not far wrong.

We declined rapidly. Attendance dropped off badly. Jimmy Piersall, who counted broadcasting among his many talents, had a sports program on a local radio station. After a game in which fans were noticeably absent from huge Municipal Stadium he said that Cleveland fans were the least loyal in the big leagues. On the day after this blast hit the air Gabe asked me to send Jimmy to his office. I didn't know why he wanted to see him nor did I care.

Gabe, it seems, gave Jimmy a stern bawling out for his attack on Cleveland fans. They were the source of the Indians' prosperity, if any, he said.

"Am I telling the truth or aren't I?" Jimmy shot back. "If I can't speak the truth on the air I may as well stop broadcasting!"

"You have no business calling our fans disloyal, whether it's the truth or not. I don't want you to insult them."

"Any time I feel like telling the truth I'm going to. I'm repeating it to you—Cleveland is the least loyal town in the big leagues!"

Which didn't sit too well with Mr. Paul.

Six weeks before the season ended storm signals went up. A Cleveland newspaper published a report that I would be released after the season. Such reports may be based on a haphazard remark over scotch and soda or they may be some newspaperman's wishful thinking. I took the report to Gabe Paul. "If you're going to let me go, let me go now," I told him. "I don't want to lose any more sleep. Put someone else in my place at once. I'm only an hour and a half from Philadelphia by air. I can sleep in my own bed tomorrow night."

"Don't pay attention to rumors," soothed Gabe.

"Mr. Paul, you and I have been around baseball for a long time. Did you ever see a report that a manager was going to get the axe when it didn't come straight from the horse's mouth?"

"The thought of dropping you has never entered my mind."

We were in fourth place that day. We were fifth on the morning the season ended. It was a Sunday morning in Los Angeles and I had just returned from church when the telephone sounded the bell of my doom.

"Gabe wants to see you," said Nate Wallack.

"I haven't had breakfast yet, Nate. I'll be with him in one hour if it's convenient for him. Otherwise I'm not available until after the game."

"You know he's the general manager, don't you?"

"I certainly do. If he's going to tell me I'm fired I can take it better on ham and eggs than on an empty stomach."

Precisely one hour later I pushed the buzzer on Gabe's door.

I heard the expected news a few minutes later: "I've got to make a change, Jimmie."

"Why didn't you make it in Cleveland six weeks ago? You knew then that you weren't going to sign me for next year. Why did you lie to me?"

More words followed, some unprintable. I walked out.

Birdie Tebbetts met Danny Murtaugh in Cincinnati during the 1961 World Series between the Reds and the Yankees. Birdie was managing the Milwaukee Braves; Danny was still piloting the Pirates. "I see that Jimmy Dykes is out in Cleveland," said Danny. "Let's toss a coin to decide which one of us puts him back in."

He flipped a quarter in the air. "Heads!" called Birdie.

The quarter hit the floor, rolled, fell flat. "Heads . . ."
Which is how I became a coach on the Milwaukee
Braves.

So there I was five months later in Bradenton,
Florida, pumping ground balls to infielders, lofting
fungoes, rounding up pitchers for jogs around the ball
park, still The Little Round Man, and feeling pretty
pooped after a day's work. I was feeling my age—
sixty-five, going on sixty-six. I could still make the low
70s on the golf links, but I was only fit for a couple
of innings in an Old Timers' ball game.

"You're too old to spend the summer under the hot
sun," said Birdie.

I exploded. "Nonsense! A man is as old as he feels
and I feel like thirty!"

"Like thirty cents, you mean."

He insisted that I could be more valuable as a super-
scout covering the major leagues and building a file on
players of the other nineteen clubs.

I put my spiked shoes and uniform away. I became
a traveling man, moving from city to city, watching
younger men play the game from a seat in the stands.
A long slow summer followed. I compared baseball in
the 1960's with the game I had played half a century
before. The file in the Braves' home office grew thicker.
The hair on my balding head grew thinner.

Birdie left the Braves at the end of the season. I was
released.

9

DISNEYLAND IN BASEBALL

I WAS NOT convinced that I was through. I could still
go eighteen holes on the links. Why couldn't I go nine
innings in a coaching job? And what would make me
feel younger than wearing "Athletics" on the shirtfront
of my uniform?

I phoned Eddie Lopat, manager of the Kansas City
version of my great old team. "You can certainly help
me," Eddie said. He cleared my hiring with Charles O.
Finley, the owner. With spring of 1963 I was mingling
with the successors to Grove, Foxx, Simmons, Cochrane
and Company in one more training camp.

Eddie posted me in the third-base coaching box. It

was a lonely spot. Not one Athletic said hello to me during a doubleheader until the eighth inning of the second game when Wayne Causey tripled. "Howdy, stranger!" I greeted him and threw an arm over his shoulders.

I became better acquainted with the fans behind third base than with my teammates. Kansas City was scoring fewer runs than the Orioles of 1954. Some even tried not to score. Bill Bryan, our occasional catcher, reached second by doubling to right. When the next runner cracked a grounder to shortstop I cupped my hands and shouted: "Stay there!" Bryan paid no attention. He lumbered to third and was out by ten feet when the shortstop threw to the third baseman.

Bryan rose from the dust and looked sheepishly at me. "Don't ask me why I did it, Jim," he said. "Give me until tomorrow to think up an excuse."

The Athletics were in a permanent slump, like the old Athletics when I first joined them. Arnold Johnson had bought the Philadelphia franchise in 1955 and transferred it to Kansas City. After his death in 1959 it had fallen into the hands of Finley, who'd made his millions in the insurance business and was determined to spend them on baseball.

Finley was a fan first and a hard-boiled baseball magnate second. He had bought a club infected with the chronic diseases of mismanagement. He resolved to cure it of its losing ways by building a major-league organization from scratch.

In the meantime, he was giving Kansas City fans a good show, if not a winner. I found myself in a fancy gold and green uniform which would have made me look like a burlesque queen if I had been a statuesque blonde of feminine persuasion. He installed a mechanical rabbit which popped up out of the ground to hand fresh baseballs to umpires. He hired a taxi to carry reliefers from the bullpen to the mound. For days he kept a Brink's truck on hand, loaded with three hundred silver dollars to be distributed to fans on the day Rocky Colavito, who was stopping over in Kansas City on his way from Detroit back to Cleveland, hit his 300th home run, which Rocky finally hit in Chicago, spoiling Finley's publicity stunt.

Sheep with fancy-colored coats roamed a pasture beyond the outfield, part of a zoo which supposedly attracted small-fry fans. We even had a live mascot, a mule which rambled around before games began.

These accessories made life on the Athletics diverting, but they had nothing to do with the serious business of winning ball games. Victories were in short supply.

It takes many years to put the pieces together that make up the jigsaw puzzle of a modern ball club. Finley was prepared to devote a lifetime and, incidentally, spend his fortune on the task. He paid his players extremely well. He scattered large sums about the map in bonuses to free agents, some in six-figure sums. He was on the telephone twenty-four hours a day with suggestions, ideas, plans, schemes, dreams. He lavished money on apparently zany stunts and collected box-office dividends on many.

One of his best ideas was the scheduling of Saturday night games at 6 P.M. The ball game would end by 9, enabling amusement-hungry fans to spend the rest of the evening at movie theaters or in downtown night clubs.

To attract fans from the rural areas of Missouri and

Kansas he staged a highly successful Farm Night. The players rode from the clubhouse to the dugout on truckloads of hay. Fans were awarded chickens, ducks, pigs and ponies. The grand rustic blowout attracted 25,000 fans to Municipal Stadium.

I honestly believe that Finley would spend his last dollar if he could find some way of putting on a uniform and managing the Athletics. To sit on the bench running his own ball club is his secret ambition. As it is, what Charlie wants he gets. I recall a meeting with General Manager Pat Friday, Manager Lopat, coaches and scouts to decide which players should be cut from the squad. We unanimously agreed that young Tom Reynolds, a good-looking outfielder and third baseman, should be sent down to the minors for more seasoning. Finley vetoed our decision. "I want to keep this boy," he said. Reynolds remained on the team.

I enjoyed coaching for the Athletics. I enjoyed the friendly comments of the fans. Kansas City loves its big-league team. Let the team climb into the first division and the sound of the noisy celebration will be heard as far away as Philadelphia.

Among the '63 Athletics was Jim Gentile, our cleanup man. Jim had become the hero of Baltimore in '61 when he hit 46 home runs. After his trade to Kansas City, Finley had offered him a $1,000 bonus for each homer.

By early September Jim had been able to drive only 28 round-trippers out of the lot. In his efforts to connect he would often overswing and lose his temper, flinging his bat, kicking dirt, hurling his helmet against the dugout wall. These tantrums caused criticism, and

Finley ordered Mel McGaha, who had succeeded
Eddie Lopat as manager, to bench him.

Gentile brought his troubles to me. He was like an
overgrown boy whose worst fault was his juvenile lack
of self-control. I quieted him down and, as all of us
baseball men do, we began to talk shop.

"You've been around a long time, Jimmie," Gentile
said. "Has the game changed much since you were a
player?"

He was fascinated as I told him about the great stars
of the Twenties, Ruth's arching homers, the power
blasts of Jimmy Foxx, the line-drive clouts of Lou
Gehrig.

"You've managed a lot of clubs, too, haven't you?"
he said.

"I sure have." And I talked about the White Sox and
Luke Appling and Zeke Bonura, happy days long in
the past.

"How old are you now, Jim?"

"Sixty . . . let's see . . . I'm sixty-seven."

"Don't you ever think of retiring?"

"I'm quitting at the end of this season."

I heard my own words with surprise. I'd never told
myself I was quitting. An inner voice had said it—and
it was true. Boy and man, I'd worn the baggy pants
and spiked shoes for more than half a century, I'd seen
baseball change from a town game played on open
lots to the spectacle it presented in the great domed
stadium in Houston. I'd done my bit in three World
Series while thousands looked on. I'd managed in many
cities, coached in others. I'd enjoyed every game, every
inning, every chance I'd handled, every hit I'd made.

If I had any regret it was that in all the years of
managing I'd never won a pennant. I'd never been

able to put the right names on the lineup card I gave the umpire. Without the right ticket you can't win the raffle. No one has yet found a way to steal first base.

It wasn't poor health that made me quit. It was the ever-changing hours of play and the psychological effects of jet travel. In the old days games began in the early afternoon, meals came at normal hours, and the nights were made for sleep. Now with day games, twi-nite games, night games, I reported at any old hour from eleven o'clock in the morning to five o'clock in the afternoon and was often in the ball park after midnight. Jet travel might be smooth and fast, but I often was in an airport long after midnight and arrived at our destination when the rest of the world was sound asleep. I recall being flown from Boston into Canada because airports in the Midwest were fogbound, and arriving in Kansas City in time to catch a few hours of broken sleep before reporting at the ball park. On that trip I wondered whether the pilot would land safely. I'd have had little to lose if we'd crashed, but the fine young men with me would have lost the best years of their lives.

Baseball was played under much the same rules as in the old days, but it was not the same game. It was no longer my dish of beans.

So the day came when it was all over. I took off my uniform with "Athletics" across the shirtfront for the last time. I heard the others saying, "Have a good winter . . . see you in the spring." I was saying "Goodbye."

It was like reaching the end of a long, winding road and going home.

10

WIVES AND OTHER WOMEN

THERE WERE seven little McMonagles who played among the bags of flour and tubs of butter in the Preston General Store. I met them all when I was sent to the store for groceries, and the fairest was Mary. She caught my eye when I was still in short pants and she held it when my teen-age adventures began. You'd have found her among the rooters when the town team played. I was her favorite, the one she cheered the loudest.

Mary was very much in my mind when I went away to Seaford. She was the first to welcome me home from Gettysburg or Atlanta and she rejoiced with me when

I finally made the Athletics. In 1920 the inevitable occurred—we got married.

My pay was $300 a month then, no bonus, no extras, no Cadillac under the table. During off-seasons I worked as a steamfitter, building muscles by carrying 6-inch pipe. Mary was the dyed-in-the-wool fan that baseball wives are supposed to be, and a mother too, bringing three children into the world, Jimmie, Jr., Charlie and little Mary. Nowadays baseball wives have gone to college and know a lot about economics; Mary left the finances to me and concentrated on our home. My pay slowly rose during the 1920's; by the time I had collected three World Series shares I had a comfortable bank balance and was able to open the bowling alleys which bore my name.

The publicity I received from playing big-league ball never affected our home life. "What was the score today?" Mary would ask, and that was the extent of her baseball talk. Evenings we'd go to the movies or I'd read a mystery novel. We were, I suppose, distressingly normal until the trade which sent me to the White Sox changed our lives. Mary and the children came to Chicago to live during the season. She had been a passionate fan, coming regularly to see me play. Her status changed after I became a manager. "I don't want you to sit with the players' wives any more," I told her. "They may think you've become unfriendly but I don't care what they think, sit by yourself. You can chat with them before or after games all you want but while the game's on be the manager's wife. The wives of players can cause a lot of trouble on any ball club. They compare salaries and when they find that one husband is being paid less than another they put a needle into their husbands when they go home. Suppose you're sitting with the wives of a pitcher and an infielder. The infielder boots one that costs the pitcher the ball game—it's been known to happen. 'Jim should have had that one,' says the pitcher's wife—and suddenly you'll be in the middle. Jim's wife resents the remark. She tells her husband and dissension starts. It's better you don't become involved. I prefer to keep out of player squabbles and so should you."

Mary took my advice and sat alone or with the children. When the kids were in their teens I sent them to camps during the summer. They broadened their knowledge of the United States by accompanying me on trips.

Mary was an ideal baseball wife.

I had no more than a nodding aquaintance with my players' wives. After I became a manager I never associated socially with them or, for that matter, with their husbands. I kept away from parties where players were invited. I didn't want to spoil their fun. I didn't want to make a player put a second highball aside for fear that I might be watching him.

At the conclusion of each White Sox training season the Elks Club of Pasadena threw a going-away party. I never attended it. I wanted the boys to enjoy a night out after long weeks of strenuous training without having Poppa's watchful eye on them.

Except for the first two springs I went to Pasadena without my family. Then I left them at home and barred the players' wives, too. I had the notion that wives would distract their husbands from the serious business of getting into shape. California was the reason, especially Hollywood with its studios, stars, the night clubs on the Strip and the then well-known sights. One year Eddie Lopat, Joe Haynes and Mike Tresh thought they'd put one over on me by smuggling their wives to the West Coast and hiding them in a Hollywood apartment. Their plot worked until the evening of our departure for the East on our three-week exhibition tour. I sent for the trio. "Gentlemen, I hope your wives have had a wonderful time in Hollywood," I said. They looked stunned. I laughed. "Don't think for a moment that I didn't know they were here. I said nothing to you because I didn't want to spoil the girls' fun."

The following spring I rescinded the ban on feminine camp followers. I took the consequences without a murmur. Players pestered me for tickets to studios and shows. I located an agent who helped me satisfy their demands. One day a player came to me with a plea: "Please, Mr. Dykes, no more tickets. I worked six hours on the diamond yesterday, then got in a little golf before dark. And then I had to take my wife out to a show you got me tickets for."

"It's better to be at a show with your wife than to carouse around the countryside with the natives, isn't it?"

"I guess it is," he admitted.

Sex seldom worms its way onto the sports pages, but it's on many a manager's mind. Healthy young athletes cannot be expected to ignore the attention which girls lavish on them. Early marriage is one way out of the dilemma. Even married men are tempted by sex-starved women while on the road. Prostitution is no longer the problem it used to be. With the passage of time, higher pay, and the expected revenue from the pension plan, players are more serious today than in the past.

11

SOME THOUGHTS ABOUT MANAGING

THE MANAGER's toughest job is not calling the right play with the bases full and the score tied in an extra-inning game. It's telling a ballplayer that he's through, done, finished. I'd rather walk on live coals with bare feet than tell a veteran, an old-timer of whom I'm personally fond, that he's over the hill and must be released. It has to be done, there's no way out. It isn't fair to send the poor guy to the general manager or president for his pink slip. The manager has to assume the responsibility himself.

You can't even offer him the hope of a comeback.

The guy may have played beside you, teamed up with you to win many a game. The curtain's going down. Statistics say he hasn't got it any more. It's tough to have to tell him so.

It's also hard to find a formula for a good-bye message to an in-betweener. In 1934 I had to close the door on a reserve outfielder who'd had three trials: with the Yankees, the Tigers, and the White Sox. I told him I was sending him to the Pacific Coast League.

"I say I'm still a big-leaguer!" he bawled. "You haven't given me a chance to play regularly here."

"Nothing would give me greater pleasure than to agree with you," I said. "Now it's your chance to prove you are right. You're going to a fast league. Act like a big-leaguer there. Make them believe you're too good for them. We'll both be happier when you come back next year."

There was no next year for him. He never returned to the majors.

In an early talk in camp each year I tried to plant the idea in the heads of my bright-eyed rookies that life in baseball is tragically short. "Right now you're going great," I'd tell them. "You'll make the team sure, you hope, and I hope so, too. But don't be discouraged if someone beats you to the job you've set your heart on. Keep trying. There may be another spot open. You're all at the starting line waiting for the gun to go off. Try to win the race by self-improvement. You win it on your own two feet. Listen to your instructors. Do as they say. You wouldn't be here at all if our scouts hadn't decided that you have big-league stuff. Have the same confidence in yourselves that they had. If you don't make it this year, consider yourselves fortunate that you're young enough to make it next.

"Don't waste your opportunities now. You must look forward to the day you'll have to take off those spiked shoes and that uniform and never wear them again. That day comes to everybody. Keep it in mind now when you're young. Don't waste time now because you have so much of it. Bear down! Heads up! Let's go . . ."

Just a corny pep talk? Not at all. It produced results more often than it failed.

How many games can a manager win for his team per season? I believe he can win from eight to fifteen if he has a strong relief corps and uses it judiciously. The twenty big-league managers of today would all get the same results from the same players. However, in today's game with its starters who lose their stuff early and its reliefers who are trained to stop rallies, the manager who knows when a starter is weakening and which reliefer to use has an advantage over his less knowledgeable rivals.

Otherwise, the difference in managers is mainly a matter of personality. Walter Alston is the self-effacing type. At the other extreme is Leo Durocher with his flaming personality. Don't mistake personality for talent. Given the same players both would get equal results in the course of a season.

I never had a standout hitter. The White Sox depended on the bunting game at a time when home-run heroes were winning pennants for other clubs. My bunting specialists were Mule Haas, Mike Kreevich and Joe Kuhel. They advanced runners into scoring position and contributed greatly to such success as we had without getting credit for it in the RBI column.

Bunting is a lost art today except for a very few specialists. I spent entire batting practice sessions trying to teach the Athletics of the early 1950's how to lay the ball down for sacrifices. The only batter who deliberately sacrifices himself is the pitcher—and how many pitchers know where to dump the ball so they will be thrown out while the runner escapes a force play? Few hitters are willing to give up a time at bat without trying to get on. A weak-hitting club—and most clubs today are weak-hitting in comparison with the slugging outfits of the past—would increase its ratio of runs to hits if it had a few experts who knew that sacrifice *means* sacrifice.

The White Sox were an underprivileged team. I used to put waiver lists under a magnifying glass in the hope of finding a phenom between the lines. The only players I could claim were rejects from other clubs. The waiver price was $7,500 then, the maximum the Sox could afford.

The nearest I came to the top was in 1936. We dashed down to the season's finale in third place, one game behind Detroit. A doubleheader with the St. Louis Browns was scheduled for that afternoon. Well, it began to rain in Chicago that morning, and the rain continued all day. Strangely enough, it didn't rain in Detroit, where the Tigers played and lost one game. If we could have won both games from the Browns, whom we'd been beating regularly all season, we'd have finished second, 19 games behind those ever-winning Yankees.

My best team flitted by so fast that I didn't realize how good they were. For seven weeks the '58 Reds displayed championship form in hitting, fielding, pitching and team spirit. Why they were in last place on the day I took charge still puzzles me. They fought their way up on their own. They were proof that sometimes undermanaging pays.

Joe McCarthy struck a perfect balance between undermanaging and overmanaging. To be sure, he had the tools, the power, strength up and down the middle, tight pitching and fine reserves. I repeat: Joe pushed a button and winning Yankees popped up year after year.

Joe won without fireworks but there was iron discipline beneath his calm exterior. He could cut up an umpire pretty good, as I heard him do when he crossed swords with Bill McGowan one day in 1936 while I stood at the plate listening. For five minutes he ripped into McGowan, splattering juicy words all over the scenery. When it was all over I raised my voice: "How come you let the manager of the Yankees get away with that kind of language?"

Despite the way his teams rolled all over my White Sox I rate Joe at the absolute top of the managerial class.

Bill McKechnie got results with as little noise as Joe McCarthy. He barely spoke above a whisper in his debates with umpires. His success was due in large part to his uncanny handling of pitchers. McKechnie could judge a pitcher's form by watching him during the warm-up. He could anticipate the moment when a pitcher was about to lose his stuff. He saved many a game by having a reliefer ready to step in at the first sign of weakness. Mac was a technical expert, smooth, unhurried, efficient.

Mickey Cochrane was an inspirational leader who set his players on fire with his own enthusiasm. His '34 Tigers had smart pitching in Tommy Bridges and

Schoolboy Rowe, and power in Hank Greenberg, but Mickey added the personal touch that welded them into a winner. Mickey spoke his mind. Anyone who failed to run out a hit didn't belong in the big leagues. He was a playing manager who really played. "As long as I can limp behind the plate, I'll catch," he said on the eve of the '34 World Series. Held together by tape, spiked in the sixth game, he spent his nights in a hospital, leaving his bed to star in each game. Mike's record was two pennants and one second-place finish in five years of managing. But for the fractured skull which ended his career, he would have been one of the greatest pilots of all time.

Which reminds me . . . although Mickey and I were close friends we battled each game to the bitter end. We insulted each other with smiles, exchanging cracks, playing tricks. One year Mickey lost the bet of a new hat to me on the White Sox's finish. I bought a wide-brimmed Stetson and sent the bill to him. It cost $20, a high price for a hat in those days. Mickey paid it, then sent me a note:

"It isn't the money, Jim. What makes me sore is wasting that big hat on a pinhead like yours."

Now, let me take off on Casey Stengel. Not on Casey's managerial talents or on his double-talk or big-time personality stuff. I blame Casey for introducing double-platooning. It was easy for Casey to double-platoon the Yankees when his bench was kept warm by utility men who were every bit as good as his regulars.

I was brought up in a time when a player wasn't taken out because the enemy pitcher was delivering the ball from the same side of the plate he hit from. He was taken out only after he'd proved he couldn't hit any

kind of pitching. The '29 Athletics would have hit anything dished up to them, from balloons to machine-gun
bullets.

I am a firm believer in the idea that the best eight
players belong in the game every day whether they're
lefties, righties or ambidextries.

Ty Cobb's statement still holds: "I can hit any ball
that's near the plate." Against southpaws Ty stood close
to the plate. He stepped back against left-handers. He
didn't take the same position in the batter's box every
time up. He adapted himself to the kind of pitching he
was facing. The pitcher had to adapt his style to Ty's.

Double-platooning hampers the development of
youngsters. A kid who sits on the bench when pitching
comes from his side of the plate cannot be taught how
to eliminate his weakness with the stick. The truly
scientific hitter learns through constant practice to meet
the ball wherever it comes from and adds valuable
points to his batting average.

I am against double-platooning. In this respect I
differ from Ol' Case', but then I never had Yankees at
my beck and call.

Today's managers are cuties. They play the game
close to the vest. They try to outsmart each other. They
change pitchers like cards in three-card monte. In the
midst of an exciting batting rally the manager calls
time, walks to the mound like a mourner bringing bad
news, holds a conference, wigwags to the bullpen. The
reliefer strolls in, goes into another conference, warms
up, has a last-minute chat with his catcher. Then, at
long last, the game is resumed. Fans who are still awake
are buying beer at the lunch counter and the others are
fast asleep.

Many of these pitching changes are caused by the

manager's desire to display himself to the TV audience as a fearless master mind. Or they're due to the manager's fear of criticism for not being the quick-witted decisive type.

During these years of my retirement I see more of Gene Mauch's managerial methods than anyone else's. Gene is still remembered as the manger who "allowed" the Phillies to lose the 1964 pennant in the season's last week. Gene didn't "allow" them to lose. They had their first and only slump of the season that week.

Gene is also criticized for acting like a little king whenever he goes on field. He's cock of the walk when his team is winning. He dies when they lose. An Astro rookie snatched away a game from the Phils with a pinch single in the ninth. Gene dashed into the clubhouse, kicked over a trayful of ribs and salad, spattering clothes hanging in lockers. His burst of temper cost him a pretty cleaning bill. This was highly explosive conduct, but to my knowledge Gene has never exploded into his players' faces. The Phils like Gene's conduct; they do their best to put that cocky victory smile on his face.

Bobby Bragan lost his job with the Braves for having too colorful a personality. Walter Alston hangs onto his job year after year although he's blah, no color, wooden, dull. Walt sits in the Dodger dugout winning pennant after pennant without saying much. But he stays on, going colorlessly along, and always does a colorful job.

I don't know whether true or false best describes the stories that circulate that Walt is Buzzy Bavasi's puppet. If they're true it's no disgrace. Bavasi knows how to find winning young players. Walt knows how to mold them into a team that wins pennants and breaks attendance records. No doubt Walt puts up a fight for his point of view when he disagrees with Buzzy, but he does it quietly, without interviews and headlines in the press.

12

HIS MAJESTY, THE UMPIRE

To LOOK at me you'd never suspect I was an umpire baiter. I'm not the baiting type. I'm not a show-off. Or an argufier who tries to think up some gag at the umpire's expense that I can slip to the gentlemen of the press and read about in tomorrow's papers.

I just went about my business, which happened to be baseball.

Yet in my time President Will Harridge of the American League charged me with "abusive behavior," with being "the John J. McGraw of our league"; and once suspended me indefinitely for describing an umpire's eyesight as less than 20/20 and his judgment as zero.

I was called the "Peacemaker" in my early days with the Athletics. I'd insert myself between an umpire and an angry teammate when an argument started and try to calm both parties down. My first real clash was purely accidental. In 1922 I executed a beautiful tag on an incoming runner only to hear the umpire call, "Safe!" I leaped up, bolted toward the gentleman in blue and unintentionally brushed against his belly. The next day Mr. Mack handed me a wire from the president's office suspending me for three days.

"Watch your step," said my manager. "You're no earthly use to me sitting in the stands in street clothes, you know."

From then on I was the umpire's dearest friend, although that atrocious decision still lurked in the back of my mind. I continued in that role after I became the White Sox manager. One spring I was elected to honorary membership in the Umpires' Association of Southern California.

Nevertheless, I found myself going into battle with the umps, although only when I knew I was right and they were wrong. They never agreed with my version of a disputed decision. They'd talk back to me, with the result that I was forced to talk back to them. I always had lots of words at my disposal. This would offend the umpire. Out I would go.

I told my Sox: "Argue with umpires if you must, but only up to a point. Don't give an umpire an excuse to put you out of the game. Play it cool until I get on the scene. I'll protect you. As soon as you hear my voice get out of range. Stand by and listen, but keep your own mouth shut."

No more than five or six Sox were sent to early showers in my thirteen years as Chicago's manager.

This doesn't mean that the Sox seldom argued. I would hop into the thick of the jawing even when I thought the player was wrong. I defended him, regardless of the cost to me. And the cost was plenty. At the beginning of each season I mailed Mr. Harridge's secretary a stack of signed checks with the amounts blank, asking him to fill them in and deposit them whenever my vocabulary sounded expensive, saving time and the cost of postage stamps for me.

I honestly believe that umpires like arguments. Jaw fests break the monotony of standing around on flat feet doing nothing for hours on end. A good lively brawl gives them the chance to display their awful power as judge, prosecutor and jury to a doubting world.

One day the White Sox knocked a Red Sox pitcher out of the box and a reliefer was sent in. He took seven warm-up pitches. "Next one's the last," I called from the bench. "Let's get going!"

George Moriarty was plate umpire. The pitcher threw an eighth pitch, a ninth, tenth, eleventh, up to a sixteenth. I ran to Moriarty. "It says in the rule book a relief pitcher can take eight warmup pitches, not sixteen!"

"Moriarty says No!" Moriarty declaimed. "And Moriarty is king around here!"

I knelt in the dust like a slave before a king and, believe it or not, I was put out of the game.

One of my dearest enemies was Cal Hubbard, who threw me out one day before I could open my big mouth. I choked on unsaid words all the way to the clubhouse, then sat down and figured out a way of speaking my piece. The next day I sidled up to Cal and said, "Throw me out, pal. I don't care. You were wrong yesterday and I'm saying it today whether you like it or not."

"Are you finished?"

"Period."

"Now you're out for today, too."

Bill Summers would listen to me with a twinkle in his eye. When I ran out of breath he'd say. "Okay, Jim. You've said your piece. Now I'll say mine. The best thing for you to do is to get out of here quietly."

And quietly I would go.

During my Cleveland career Hal Trosky once slid back to first on a pick-off throw. His foot was caught in the bag but Steve Basil called him out. I ran from the bench past Summers, who was officiating at the plate. "Don't argue with Basil," Summers warned as I went by.

"I just want to find out if Trosky hurt his ankle," I explained.

By the time I arrived at first base Trosky had scrambled to his feet and was being waved to the bench by Basil. I told the umpire what I thought of his decision. He answered in kind. We stood jawing toe to toe until he cut me short with a wave of his arm. "Out!" he bawled.

Slowly I retreated. "I told you not to argue," said Summers, with a shake of his head. "When will you ever learn?"

I learned later that my jawing bout had cost me $150, a high price to pay for a vocal exercise.

Much as I admired Summers I couldn't resist ribbing him occasionally. The spring I coached for the Pirates he was calling 'em off first base in an exhibition game with the Reds at Tampa when he got into a debate with one of my teammates. I stayed out of it until the argument ended, then shouted, "Same old Summers! Booting 'em as usual!"

He whipped his arm up in the oust sign. "Put on your boots when you take your shower and keep your brains dry!" he shouted back. It was the only time he tossed me out in his years of umpiring.

Bill McGowan issued his edicts loud and clear, and didn't like to be interrupted while giving them. Even the strongest man has a weakness, and I discovered Mac's. He was betting on the horses. Mac wasn't a big gambler, oh, no! He laid two bucks every day on the daily double.

Games began at 1:30 P.M. in those days. Race tracks, of which we had many in Chicago, ran off the first half of the double at 2 P.M. I let Mac believe that I was getting racing results over a radio in the clubhouse, which was not precisely true—there was no radio in the clubhouse and no means of getting information to the bench if there had been one. But I gave Mac the thumbs-down sign at 2:10 to indicate that his horse had lost. It was my way of needling an otherwise nerveless umpire who'd roar me down whenever I opened my mouth. My trick worked until the day he hit a daily double on the nose.

Years later, when I was managing the Athletics, Eddie Robinson, our first baseman, got into an argument with McGowan. I wasn't involved but I believed McGowan was wrong, for Robinson rarely protested a call. Our games were being televised, which gave me an opportunity to pull another trick on my old opponent.

When the next inning began I remarked: "You sure blew that decision on Robinson, Mr. McGowan."

"What do you know about it?" he snapped.

I gestured in the direction of the Athletics' office on the top tier of the grandstand. "They saw it upstairs in a close-up shot on TV."

"Who saw it? Was it Mr. Mack?"

"I won't tell you."

McGowan was a conscientious umpire and my remark still troubled him as I met him at the next day's pregame conference at the plate. "Come on now, Jim," he said. "Who said I blew that Robinson call yesterday?"

"Everyone in Philadelphia." He looked so crestfallen that, for the first time in my life, I took pity on an umpire. "Forget it," I said. "I was ribbing you."

He turned scarlet. "You blankety-blank so-and-so!" he roared and would have sent me packing if the game had been on. It was one of the few times I had the satisfaction of needling one of the game's most scrupulous umpires.

All catchers question ball and strike calls now and then. McGowan would tolerate a mild beef from a veteran receiver, but he quickly took the freshness out of a rookie. "Busher!" he'd say. "You do the catching and leave the umpiring to me!"

"Ball one!" McGowan announced as a pitch came in at knee level in a 1950 game with the Red Sox.

"What's that?" mildly inquired Sammy White, then a Boston rookie.

"Wash out your ears!" growled McGowan. "I said 'Ball' in big-league English."

Later in the game White dared question Bill's call of a low outside curve. Up went McGowan's arm. "Out, busher, out!" he roared. It was his way of initiating a newcomer into big-league manners and, incidentally, the quickest ouster I ever saw.

While I was managing Cleveland, in a game at Detroit umpire Larry Napp called an Indian runner safe on a close play at first base. Norm Cash, the Tiger first sacker, kicked up a fuss and his manager, Bob Scheffing, came on the field to back him up. During the confusion my runner took off for second. Cash's quick throw cut him down.

I ran protesting to Napp. "Don't you know the rules?" I demanded. "You should have called time. There was a tenth man on the field when Cash made that throw."

"I didn't see any tenth man," said Napp.

"How about Scheffing?"

"He was in foul territory."

I appealed to the other umpires. They admitted that Scheffing had been on the field, but they refused to interfere unless Napp asked them to. I ran back to Napp. He refused to change his decision.

Before the next day's game I took three lineup cards to the conference at the plate. I gave one to Scheffing, one to the announcer, and one to Napp. Napp put his card in his pocket without looking at it. Scheffing glanced at his and noticed that I'd written ten names on it. He started to say something but I winked, put a finger to my lips, and he kept quiet.

"Is my lineup okay, Mr. Napp?" I inquired with an innocent expression on my face.

He drew the card from his pocket and looked at it. "What's the idea of ten men on this card, Jim?"

"Suppose you tell me. The Tigers had ten men on the field yesterday, didn't they? And you let them get away with it. If it was legal then, it's legal now ——"

"Like Bejesus it is! I got a mind to put you out of the game!"

I burst into laughter, then produced three correct lineup cards. "I think I've made my point," I said, and walked away before he could make good on his threat.

Philadelphia had its Sunday blue laws, Boston had a seven P.M. Sunday curfew. We dropped the first game of a Sunday doubleheader to the Red Sox and were tied, 0 to 0, in the ninth inning of the nightcap. Down we went, one, two, three.

Then . . . craaackk! The first Red Sox in the bottom of the ninth lined a double to left. I glanced at the clock. It was 6:40. If the run scored before curfew rang we'd lose two games and return to Comiskey Park tails between our legs.

"Time!" I yelled, and slowly walked to the mound. "You've pitched a great game," I told my starter. "Suppose you argue with me."

"What for?"

"I'm taking you out and you don't want to go."

We wasted a minute in double-talk, then I grabbed the ball and waved to the bullpen. When the new pitcher arrived I said, "Take your time. And walk the next man up."

He got my angle. He tossed his eight warm-up throws, then obediently walked the batter.

Up I jumped again. "Time!"

I had the legitimate excuse of wildness for relieving pitcher No. 2. I waved No. 3 in. "This next batter is going to bunt," I told him. "No matter where he lays it down, make the play at first base."

It was 6:43. At 6:44 the batter bunted. The ball went to the right of the mound; the pitcher fielded it and threw to first.

I jumped up. "Out you go!" I yelled, waving my arm toward the bullpen.

Now it was the turn of Joe Cronin, the Red Sox manager, to leap up, rush to the plate, and accuse me of stalling.

"Atta boy, Joe!" I chirped. "Keep at it! Keep kicking!"

Joe stopped in the middle of a sentence and got off the field. I looked at the clock. It was 6:52.

My third reliefer was on hand. "Walk this batter," I said.

Obediently he flipped four wide tosses. The bases were full.

I walked slowly to the mound but Umpire Cal Hubbard was already in the outfield, waving to the bullpen. Onto the field came southpaw Jake Wade. "No, no, no!" I yelled. "I don't want a southpaw! Get me Pete Appleton."

"You waved your left arm," said Hubbard. "You either pitch Wade or I'll forfeit this game!"

I was stymied. A forfeit would not only cost us the game but it would cost the White Sox a thousand-dollar fine and I didn't know whether they had that much money in the bank.

I still had a card up my sleeve. I approached Ed Rommel, who'd been calling balls and strikes. "Have I told you that Wade is my pitcher, Ed?" I asked my old Athletic teammate.

"No, you haven't."

"Isn't it true that no one is officially in the game until the manager informs the umpire-in-chief, who happens to be you?"

"That's right."

"That's all I want to know."

Wade didn't play my stalling game. He threw his warm-up pitches so quickly that it was still 6:59 by the clock when Lou Finney stepped up to the plate for the Red Sox. Wade laid one over. Finney stroked a fly to center. The winning run scored. Just as the runner came home I looked at the clock. The minute hand jumped to exactly 7 o'clock.

"Curfew! Curfew!" I yelled. "That run don't count!"

No one heard me. The umpires were already off the field.

All of which means that you can't beat the law, however foolish it is. We lost the game; I lost $250, the price for what the umpires called "deliberate stalling" in their report to the league office.

I couldn't resist a dig at that crew of tale-telling umpires. When next we visited Washington Cal Hubbard was the umpire-in-chief. I'd had my run-ins with Cal, and I sent coach Mule Haas to the plate conference with the lineup cards.

"What's going on here?" asked Hubbard. "Dykes has only put eight names on this card."

"He says you picked his pitcher for him in Boston the last time around, so he's letting you do it today!"

Mule never told me what Hubbard's next words were. I bet they weren't quotable.

Bill Guthrie hailed from Chicago's South Side and talked with a "dese, dem and dose" accent. Bill broke into arbitrating in the 1920's when I was young and cocky. He called a Detroit runner out at the plate on a very close play. I sprinted in from third base, screaming.

"Back to de bag if you don't wanna get t'rown out!" he bellowed, heaving his bull-like chest at me. I brought up short and faded away.

I liked Bill, who let you know precisely where you stood in a very few words. The next time I went to the plate I turned to Johnny Bassler, the Tiger catcher. "This is getting to be a great league, John," I said. "You need a formal introduction before you can speak to an umpire."

Guthrie stepped in front of me, whipped off his mask and stuck his jaw in my face. "Look, kid," he said in a firm voice, "you ain't gonna need no card of introduction to get in the shower room. Shut up! Get me?"

Bill operated on the theory that a player had the right to say his piece and then "Shut up and stay shut." Early in his career he got into a dispute with Whitey Witt, the Yankee lead-off man. Whitey said his piece, then failed to shut up. Miller Huggins, the pint-sized Yankee manager, came running to back him up. "Out ya go, Witt!" ordered Guthrie. He pointed a finger at Huggins. "And take da bat boy with ya!"

Which ended the discussion for the day.

I felt the sting of Guthrie's tongue when he called a strike on a pitch under my chin. I wasn't going to kick. I turned my head and looked down, hoping to sneak a glance at the catcher's next sign.

"What's the matter, kid?" said Guthrie. "Got a doubt in your mind on that last one?"

"No," I replied, "I wasn't going to criticize you, but since you mentioned it, wasn't that last one a little high?"

"If your eyesight's gettin' poor, kid, don't worry. No one's gonna know but you, me and the catcher."

During my White Sox days Taft Wright chased a fly into left-field foul territory, where Cleveland's bullpen was located. Several Indian players got in his way and the ball fell safe. I protested to Harry Geisel, the umpire-in-chief, who turned his back on me. I ran to Steve Basil at third base, who said he'd seen no interference.

I blew up with a loud bang. I'm afraid I wasn't as polite as I should have been. I used some pretty strong words, such as "blind," "outrage," "foul play," and a few others of the four-letter variety. This was no ordinary mistake in judgment. Everyone in the ball park must have seen Wright stumble into a Cleveland player just as he was about to catch the ball—that is, everyone but the umpires.

They were deaf as well as blind. Basil finally silenced me with a magnificent swoop of his arm. I muttered under my breath all the way to the clubhouse.

The following day President Harridge suspended me indefinitely, accusing me of "using obscene and abusive language, attempting to bulldoze and humiliate umpires, delaying the game, and general offensiveness."

I fought back against this cruel and unusual punishment. I fired a broadside at Harridge in a statement to the press. Why hadn't I been given a hearing? Even a man accused of murder is given a chance to defend himself in court. Where was justice? And where were the umpires' eyes?

Then I dressed myself in my Sunday best, stuck a straw hat on my head, a long black cigar in my mouth, and haunted the umpires from a rocking chair at the extreme end of the left-field foul line until my term in the hoosegow ended.

My Athletics were riding high when we visited Yankee Stadium in 1952. Harry Byrd had pitched a great game but he was trailing Allie Reynolds 1 to 0, as the ninth inning opened. Then, with one out, we filled the bags on two walks and an infield hit.

Joe Astroth was up. He took three straight balls. One more wide one and the game would be tied.

The next pitch was a called strike.

Reynolds then delivered a ball above the letters. Astroth dropped his bat and started toward first. Umpire Ed Hurley had hesitated on the call. Now he announced: "Strike!"

"What?" gasped Astroth. "That was a mile high!" Our coaches, Wally Moses at first and Tom Oliver at third, came charging toward the plate. From the dugout stormed General Dykes followed by his entire army of benchwarmers. For five minutes the air was full of words aimed point-blank at Hurley. Hurley hurled 'em right back at us. It was a standoff. I called off my troops. The decision stood. It was two strikes, three balls.

Reynolds faced Astroth again. He fired a fast ball over the heart of the plate. "Strike three!" Two were out.

Then Allie Clark hit an easy fly to Mickey Mantle in center field. The game was over. We'd lost to the Yankees again. More important to me was the loss of a chance to take third place.

In my frustration I popped off good. "Hurley choked up," I told the writers. "He's a home-town umpire, a Yankee-lover. Sure, the Yanks want to win the pennant again, but they don't want it handed 'em on a silver platter."

No one was fined or suspended for that noisy protest

on a questionable ball-and-strike decision. It couldn't
happen today. Now there's a rule outlawing kicks on
balls and strikes, the penalty instant ousting. This ain't
baseball. It ain't even cricket. If baseball is worth playing at all, it's worth playing for keeps. I and nobody
else has ever got an umpire to reverse himself on a
ball-and-strike call. But I believe kicks should be made
if only to keep an umpire on his toes.

Umpires knew that I was on the ball, ready to raise
heck whenever they slipped up. Those who tried to
silence me knew they couldn't. In the heat of some
arguments I often got profane. But whoever said that
men playing a man's game must be nice Nellies is a
sissy. I wasn't nice. I was defending my rights.

I respect umpires. They live hard, lonely lives. They
try to give honest decisions. But they are human beings
and make mistakes.

When a ballplayer who represents the winning run is
called out on a close decision and doesn't kick, the fans
think he doesn't care. When he stages a protest the
fans know he cares. Kicking is evidence of the player's
sincere devotion to the interests of his team. It adds
dramatic excitement to games. The player who takes
hairline decisions lying down doesn't belong in a big-
league uniform. I like to see a guy jump up, stick his
jaw in the umpire's face and let loose. A good argument
wakes up the umpire. It wakes up the fans. It's part of
the color of baseball.

The leagues have stopped all that today. You don't
see that hell-bent-for-breakfast attitude any more, the
runner bouncing up from a slide to let the umpire—
and the fans—know that he's willing to give an arm
and a leg to win a ball game.

Old-time umpires took protests for granted. Some

became famous for their ways of handling unruly players. Today's umpires cow players into silence. There were times when Jimmy Piersall got the thumb before he opened his mouth.

I was neither an umpire baiter nor an umpire hater. As long as they called 'em where I saw 'em they were among my best friends.

13

IT'S ONE HECK OF A JOB

EVERY BALLPLAYER has a price tag on him. He can be sold for cash or traded for a player or players of equivalent value.

The manager has no price on his head. He's the creature of whim or reputation. He's hired for a variety of reasons, some of which have little to do with his big baseball brain. He is also fired for a variety of reasons, some of which have nothing to do with his team's record or his managerial ability.

No season passes without several managers getting the gate. It's been happening since the beginning of baseball time. I don't think it will ever end.

Firing a manager often has nothing to do with the stated reasons. Don Heffner was whisked away from a job as coach for the New York Mets to manage the Cincinnati Reds in 1966. After a few months he was summarily tossed into the cold and publicly labeled a failure. The Reds were then in the second division, not because of Don's misdeeds but because Frank Robinson, the club's leading hitter, had been traded away by Bill DeWitt before Don had met the '66 Reds for the first time.

There are only twenty managerial jobs in the big leagues. Once fired, a man has small chance of connecting elsewhere. Even success is no guarantee of keeping a job. Rogers Hornsby gave St. Louis its first modern pennant and world's championship in 1926 and was on his way before the next season opened. Lou Boudreau was the toast of Cleveland in 1948 and gone two years later. Charlie Dressen won the 1953 flag for the Dodgers and was fired a few weeks after the season ended for demanding a two-year contract. 1964 was a bad year for the flag-winning pilot Yogi Berra. You can lose a job by winning. It ain't fair.

On the other hand, managers are usually hired to restore losing clubs to health. In most cases they sign one-year contracts. It's impossible for a manager to produce results in a single season. Three years are needed to prove that a manager has found the winning combination. The first year should be devoted to a study of the team's weaknesses and needs. New players should be fitted into the pattern during the second year. By the third year the manager should be able to improve the team's standing. Only then can his talents be fairly judged.

The manager is the creature of the man who hires

him, either the owner or the general manager. They hold the purse strings. The general manager has the power to obtain new players. Unless the manager has the authority to make deals, as I did with the White Sox, the poor guy is at the mercy of his front office. Too often it's the general manager who should be fired for not providing the required players, not the field manager who's doing the best he can with the material at hand.

The relationship between manager and general manager should be close, but the limits of their authority should be sharply defined. The general manager should never interfere with the manager's handling of players and he should be careful about criticizing the manager's decisions during play. He should inform the manager about negotiations for players and give the manager the right to veto deals.

The manager and general manager should act as a team within the team. Buzzy Bavasi and Walt Alston are a prime example of successful harmony between front office and dugout. Another successful partnership is that of George Selkirk and Gil Hodges. With Gil's co-operation George has obtained players who lifted the Washington Senators from tenth place to eighth in three seasons, while Gil has given Washington fans a sound, hustling team.

Managers are hired with cameras whirring and reporters' pencils poised. They are often fired without explanation and in a most mysterious way. Managers strain to catch hints about their future as their contracts near the end. The general manager's "vote of confidence" is regarded as a sure sign that the axe is being sharpened for the manager's head. If he visits the press club after games, the manager may hear a newsman's remark and the secret is out. If he's managing a loser he just smells firing in the air.

One September day in 1954 I was putting my pants on in the Orioles' clubhouse when Ed Munzel of the Chicago *Sun-Times* came up. "What goes around here?" he asked in a manner of greeting.

"Dykes," I said.

Munzel wheeled about and took off for his typewriter. It was the shortest interview on record.

I'd known that my time was up that morning when I caught a glimpse of Paul Richards in the Southern Hotel, where he'd been smuggled. Three mornings later, between orange juice and eggs, Paul confirmed my guess by saying that he'd been hired to pick up the pieces of the Baltimore disaster in '55. "How about you?" he asked. "What are your plans?"

"I want no connection with the club next year," I told him, looking him straight in the eye.

My departure from Baltimore was quick. The season's final game ended at 4:30 that Sunday afternoon. I dressed, grabbed my bags and was on a train to Philadelphia by 5 o'clock. I ate dinner at home.

The manager has no private life from the moment he signs his contract. He is on display every day from the moment he arrives in the ball park until he hops into his car after the game. He is on call at every other moment, sometimes in the middle of the night. Awake or groggy with sleep he must be able to think straight; his every word is quotable, his every act reportable.

He must create a public image, be the symbol of the city his club represents. The image must be that of a colorful public servant with a high sense of civic responsibility. He must be charming with women, tender with children and, of course, a man's man, humble yet bold, retiring yet aggressive, cautious yet daring. Although he has never taken a lesson in public speaking he must make public speeches with lots of laughs and wise sayings in them like "Nice guys finish last."

He must also be a psychologist who can read the minds of the players under his control. He must be able to hold the hands of the jittery ones and be able to paste the bold ones in the nose when they get out of line.

And, by the way, he must know baseball, come up with snap decisions and never lose his head when things go wrong.

It's one heck of a job.

And, also by the way, he must be able to get along with his club owner and general manager or it's curtains for him, fare thee well . . .

A manager must also be able to get along with the newspapermen assigned to cover his club. In no other enterprise is the manager under closer observation by the press than in big-league ball. At any minute of night or day he may be asked why he didn't zig when he zagged, or vice versa. And he'd better come up with the right answer.

Dependent upon the number of local and suburban papers published in any given city, from four to ten writers rush to the manager's office or locker room after the game and proceed to quiz him. If his team happens to have just lost a tight ball game he squirms with impatience as he climbs into long johns in the presence of the persistent gentlemen of the press.

Baseball writers aren't what they used to be. Thirty years ago they wrote breezy firsthand reports of the game, making the players bigger than in life, each game as historical a struggle as the battle of Yorktown or Gettysburg. They dubbed John J. McGraw the "Little Napoleon." They crowned Babe Ruth as "King of Swat." They were keen reporters and fervent fans.

Broadcasting has changed baseball writing. Today the writers scrape a manager's brains for angles that the broadcasters have overlooked in their pregame, play-by-play or postgame shows. They dish up the brains as their own and serve them in their morning or afternoon papers.

The manager who objects to spending fifteen or twenty minutes with the writers, no matter how weary he feels, is risking his job, for the writers have the power to smash his public image and make him seem inept, if not a fool. No manager will last long if he antagonizes the press. A blunder in a press conference can do far more harm than an error with the bases full in a game. Only a manager with an overpoweringly strong club can afford to close his door to the press. Most clubs are not constructed that way; they battle through game after game, lose some, win others. Most managers look forward to the postgame conference with distaste, misgivings and, sometimes, as a pain in the neck. But they can't get rid of it.

Managing was paradise when I broke in in 1934. I had no press conference after games. Morning-paper writers stayed in the press box to bang out their stories. Writers for the afternoon sheets hurried to their offices, their stories in mind. The game was the thing, how played, how won or lost, with little or nothing about behind-the-scenes incidents and few, if any, direct quotes from the manager. Only in recent years has television robbed newspapermen of objective reporting and forced them to dig into the manager's mind for angled stories.

My relations with writers were excellent. When I went to Detroit in 1959 I told the local newsmen: "You fellows are baseball experts. You know as much about the game as anyone. If you've got some general questions about my strategy, ask me. I'll try to tell you what was on my mind. If you disagree with me stick to your own opinions. Publish what you think. I shan't blame you. You have your job. I have mine." This was my theory about the relations between a manager and the press and it worked.

I told the writers the exact truth. Sometimes, as at the winter meetings, it wasn't easy to know what the exact truth was. One of the favorite pastimes of newsmen during the off-season is to cook up imaginary deals. When they'd ask me about mine I'd smile and say: "If you believe it, write about it." That served to end many an interview.

John Carmichael of the Chicago *Daily News* got me into difficulties with the rest of the local press by guessing right during the 1937 meetings. I was trying to trade pitcher Vern Kennedy and Dixie Walker to Detroit for Gerald Walker, Marv Owen and Birdie Tebbetts. Mickey Cochrane refused to let Birdie go. Carmichael published a "dream trade" story which was exactly that. Eventually I made a deal with the Tigers by their substituting Mike Tresh, then with Toledo, a Tiger affiliate, for Birdie. When I announced the deal the other Chicago writers accused me of favoritism toward Carmichael. It was a tight squeeze, explaining that Johnny had practised some kind of mental telepathy on me.

Two of my White Sox got into a noisy argument over a play, in the clubhouse after a game. They were cussing each other out but I let them go to it, for I knew that ballplayers never come to blows. Finally I walked over and told them to cut out the nonsense and the row ended. Meantime, several writers had dropped into the clubhouse. The following day stories about dissension on the club appeared.

There was no dissension on the club; the argument had merely been the blowing off of steam. I issued an order closing the clubhouse door to newsmen for a fifteen-minute cooling-off period. This didn't sit well with Jimmy Gallagher, the live-wire representative of the Chicago *American,* who began to publish daily columns in which I was depicted as a small-time Hitler, bent on suppressing the freedom of the press. For ten days Gallagher continued to depict poor Jimmie Dykes, who really loved everybody, as a villain with a little black mustache over his upper lip.

Gallagher would come down to the bench before games and sit with me, as friendly as ever. I'd needle him and he would needle me back. Finally I said, "Jimmy, as long as you keep attacking me that door is going to stay closed." Then I quickly changed the subject.

About a week later I bought the bulldog edition of the *American* and turned to the sports page. Not one mention of Jimmie Dykes was in Gallagher's column. The next day I cornered him. "Jim," I said, "the freedom of the press is safe in Comiskey Park from now on. The clubhouse door will stay unlocked twenty-four hours a day. Come in. Enjoy yourself. There'll be ringside seats for the next battle royal between the White Sox."

Jim laughed. It was my last run-in with the fourth estate.

I even escaped the sharpshooters, those sports col-

umnists who specialized in sharp digs and caustic comment. In fact I won the applause of Colonel Egan, the
Boston *American's* typewriter wielder, who dipped his
ribbons in poison ink. Egan had taken off against the
Braves' management in 1943 for releasing Tony Cuc-
cinello, a hot favorite wherever he played. Tony came
to me and asked if I could use a veteran second sacker.

"Not today," I said. "But tomorrow I can. Don Kollo-
way is going in the Army."

Egan lauded me to the skies for saving Tony from
oblivion. What he didn't know was that I had taken
Cucc' to save my own forty-seven-year-old legs from
going back to work.

It was a lucky move. Cucc' played great ball for me,
losing the American League batting title to George
Stirnweiss in 1945 by three little points.

Baseball writers have their pressures, too. Among my
friends of the press was Dan Daniel, long with the
New York *World-Telegram.* Dan surprised me by coming to the defense of modern ballplayers in a reply to
Ty Cobb, who had stated in a national weekly that old-
timers were superior in all departments of play.

I tackled Dan on his counterblast, with which I dis-
agreed, on my next trip to New York. "You don't really
mean what you said in your reply to Cobb, do you?"

He looked me in the eye and saw I wasn't kidding.
In that abrasive voice which sometimes got into his
stories he said, "Of course not, Jimmie, but I've got to
live with the Yankees."

14

DO-IT-YOURSELF BASEBALL

Speaking of old-timers, which I'm going to do now, they were superior to modern players because they did it themselves. Any time you do something yourself it's because you want to do it. In other words, we old-timers had *desire*.

Many of the famous big-leaguers of the 1920's were veterans of World War I. They hailed from all parts of the United States, the most numerous being from my native state of Pennsylvania. Baseball offered young men an escape from the dullness of small-town life. We were guaranteed a good wage and gained local and national recognition. It was great, reading your name in the box scores.

Among the Pennsylvanians in baseball were the sons of coal miners from the northwestern part of the state, Steve O'Neill and Bucky Harris the most prominent. Both starred, both became managers. Harris gained fame as the "boy wonder" when he led the Washington Senators to the World's Championship in the tingling 1924 World Series over John J. McGraw's New York Giants, at the age of twenty-seven.

I grew up at a time when America was still a land of wide-open spaces in cities as well as the countryside. Any bunch of boys could seize a vacant lot or field and transform it into a diamond by their own efforts. In Preston we cleared a field of weeds and stones, lugged flat rocks into place as bases and used an unanchored wooden slab as home plate. Our first baseballs were made of tightly wound twine with glove leather as covers. We saved hard-earned pennies to buy bats and gloves at the general store and induced our mothers to make uniforms for us. Our team was adopted by the town as its own, and as we grew older we flung challenges to the whole world.

We were out on the diamond from morning to night, teaching ourselves how to hit, run, field and throw, and picking up tricks of the game from semipros or by reading about Athletics or Phillies games. We were strictly on our own; no one coached us, no adults were present. I learned how to field shots that took eccentric bounces on the rocky infield, gaining that nimbleness which served me well in later years. I used a batting stance that came natural to me; I learned how to connect solidly with the rough fuzzy ball. I wasn't fast, but I learned how to break for first with the crack of the bat and how to save steps rounding the bases. I learned I had to steal on the pitcher, not the catcher, and how to slide under an infielder's tag. I learned how to go back for pop-ups, how to get off an accurate throw as a runner crashed into me. I learned how to make and to break up double plays. I learned all these fundamentals because I loved to play baseball and played it at every opportunity. If I had any weakness when I became a professional it was against the curve ball, especially when it came in with two strikes against me. This was a natural weakness, for I was not a good hitter.

When we played together long enough to gain an identity, fans crowded around our unfenced field. At big games with nearby nines the entire male population of Preston and adjoining communities was present. They stood along the foul lines in the outfield and behind a wire netting stretched on poles behind the plate. They tossed back fouls that dropped among them, for they knew we seldom had more than three or four balls per game. We passed the hat for contributions and bought regulation bats, gloves and shoes. Our pitchers learned to control a regulation ball, how to make it drop, incurve, outcurve. We were on our way to a distant goal, for every one of us was aiming for a try-out with the Athletics or the Phillies.

Pennsylvania teemed with ball clubs like ours. Every town and crossroads on the Main Line had its home-grown team. A step above us were the semipro teams, many of which represented large enterprises and were organized in industrial leagues. Baseball was the thing. It was fun. It worked off juvenile energies. We came from working-class families. We had no hope of going to college; many of us never finished high school.

The national game was our main interest. It offered a chance of becoming somebody in later life. And it was the greatest sport invented by man.

And our own.

We were called "country boys," because Preston was a village. When we were strong enough to take on all comers we challenged slickers from the city. My father and a Mr. Wolfenden, whose first name I forget, gave us the name of Penn Street Boys and handled scheduling and necessary business details. They arranged a game with the Victrix club from the city, which attracted an enormous crowd, four thousand at least.

When the Victrix manager saw that we were mere kids from fourteen to seventeen years old he called us a bunch of "babies" and wanted to cancel the game. My father said, "I'll make you a proposition. If you beat us we'll give you fifty bucks. If you lose you get nothing. How about it?"

We outslicked Victrix by a score of 21 to 1.

Encouraged by this easy triumph my father sought other winner-take-all games and booked one with the strong Irish-Roman Benevolent Union team from Ardmore. Several thousand fans cheered our every move. Lefty Forbes, our little southpaw, had a snappy curve and lots of guts. We beat the bigger, older guys, 7 to 2.

I played anywhere in the infield. I was sure-handed and had a strong arm. The IRBU team offered me fifty cents a game plus a dime for the fare to Ardmore and return. I jumped, played a few games, and then jumped to Garrett Hill, which offered me a whole dollar a game.

I was getting into the big money. To make sure of winning a big game before a big crowd Garrett Hill offered $25 to Jack Nabors, the Athletics pitcher who still holds the club record for total bases on balls, to start for us. Our opponents recognized Nabors as a ringer. In the course of a hot argument they were forced to admit that their own pitcher was a ringer from the Phillies. Both of the pros were barred and the game went on with clean lineups. We won, I recall, by something like 7 to 5.

My reputation as a steady infielder spread. When I was fifteen Strawbridge & Clothier Department Store offered me $50 to play two week-end games in the industrial league to which its team belonged. Every large business enterprise sponsored baseball in those days. The players were on the firm's payroll, appearing three or four times a week in "Twilight League" games which began at 5 P.M. Industrial leaguers were the aristocrats of semipro ball; their play compared favorably with that of the lower minor leagues in organized ball. Bill Morgan, star pitcher of the Pennsylvania Railroad team, could easily have made the Athletics if he had tried. Jack Lapp, the big catcher from Mervyn, actually was signed by Mr. Mack and spent nine years with the Athletics.

My next step up the ladder came from Monte Cross, the Athletics' shortstop from 1902 to 1907, who offered me the second-base spot on the Seaford, Delaware, team which he was managing. I'd never lived away from home; I longed to see the world. Seaford was in a four-club semipro circuit. My pay for three games a week would be $15, board and room. I packed a bag and boarded a southbound train.

At Seaford I was in fast company. My shortstop partner was none other than Joe Boley, who was to occupy a similar post on the three-time Athletic champions.

Our leading pitcher was Ed Rommel, lean and juvenile, whose knuckleball was to fool American leaguers for Mr. Mack for so many years. And among our umpires was Bill McGowan, who came over from his Wilmington home to officiate.

Many a time in later years Boley, Rommel and I reminisced about our Seaford days, the pretty girls we squired, the deep hotel mattresses, the huge meals, especially the crisp Southern fried chicken, and the funny incidents on our automobile trips to Milford, Salisbury and Cambridge, the other towns on the circuit. Each team had eight regulars, three pitchers, and an extra catcher. We'd play despite bruises, muscle strains or upset stomachs caused by overeating that wonderful hotel food. It was great to be young and a ballplayer!

At Seaford Mike Dresnan found me and sent me on my way to Shibe Park.

My long amateur and semipro experience equipped me with the ability to solve any baseball problem. I could play any position and knew what to do in any situation. No one taught me; I developed my own skills.

In this respect I was no different from other big-leaguers of that day. We all made use of our natural ability. We were self-reliant, independent, driven on by the intense desire to be the best. That's why there were so many fine players in the 1920's, among them superior athletes whose names are still remembered for their feats.

We took things as they were. We didn't have air-conditioned clubhouses with wall-to-wall carpeting on the floors. We hung our street clothes in narrow open lockers, trod bare boards. We had no white-tiled trainer's quarters; we took our aches to a corner of the clubhouse where the trainer rubbed us down with plenty of elbow grease.

The showers trickled tepid water. Playing in St. Louis on a sizzling summer day was like being given a slow broil under a grill; we put wet cabbage leaves on our heads between innings to avoid sunstroke. We rushed to the hotel after games to lie in tub baths to soak off the sweat—the hotel had no showers. Shibe Park had the smallest and most uncomfortable clubhouse in the league. There was more space in the Polo Grounds, where we played the Yankees until 1923, but it was no better equipped.

Yet we stayed in good condition. Conditioning was a matter of personal pride and self-discipline. I took on weight during the off-season and spent the first week of training moaning and groaning it off. My only self-indulgence was for beer. Mr. Mack wouldn't stand for hard liquor and made an example of any tippler who came his way.

Before Prohibition, beer was dispensed in the Shibe Park grandstand. The fans' clothes were catch-as-catch-can. Boys crowded into the two-bit bleachers. Baseball was cheap, dramatic entertainment under the summer sun, which is the best way to watch and to play the game.

Shibe Park had single-decked wooden stands. A 15-foot wall enclosed the outfield. Fans watched games free from the rooftops of houses on Twentieth Street. Mr. Mack tried to buy the houses, but the owners jacked up the price so he blocked off the free-viewers' view by raising the wall to 40 feet.

The starting time of ball games was 3:15 P.M. We'd burn up if a game lasted after 5:30. We players lived regular lives, ate regular meals, enjoyed sleep at regular hours. Not even our longest road trip, from Philadelphia to St. Louis, disturbed our daily schedule.

The train would leave early in the evening, rookies and utility men in upper berths, veterans and regulars below. We'd play cards or talk baseball in our two private cars, keeping our minds on our business, which was baseball.

Road trips were adventures in high living for boys who'd grown up in small towns or on farms. We lived at the club's expense in the best hotels, slept in luxurious beds and caught fascinating glimpses of sophisticated living. Lobby-sitting might be the favorite way of wasting off-hours for some, but I'd go browsing around, dropping into a speakeasy now and then for a glass of spiked Prohibition beer, more in curiosity than for a drink at a buck a throw. I wanted to see for myself what went on behind those peepholes in closed doors. I'd come away, satisfied that I'd seen a slice of real high life.

The big moment of each day on the road came when I opened a napkin in the hotel dining room and looked into the waiter's face. "What'll it be, heavy or light?" the Irish waiter would ask in Boston's Brunswick Hotel. I'd order "heavy," meaning chowder, a steak or a lobster, plenty of French fries, a fancy salad, a creamy dessert and coffee. Then I'd sigh with satisfaction as I signed the check. I'd go out, feeling like a lord, knowing I'd have to work off that meal in the ball park the next day.

Women were harder to resist on the road than the cup that supposedly cheers. Girls would spot a player at the ball park and call him up at the hotel afterward. In every city on the circuit certain unmarried boys had a girl friend or two. Smuggling girls into hotel rooms led Mr. Mack to put his foot down on the practice. "You wouldn't bring a slut into your home, would you?" he'd say. "Well, your hotel room is your home on the road. Keep it clean." He was strict in cracking down on casual affairs. I wouldn't say they never happened. I've seen it myself.

Later I understood Mr. Mack's viewpoint. When I became a manager I fixed the price of careless love at $500 to anyone getting careless, and this remained the price wherever I went. I tried to keep a close check on my players, but it was a losing game. Girl sees ballplayer, phones for a date, and not even the sharpest private eye can keep them from getting together. The midnight curfew is the only regulation the manager can resort to. But a coach's rap on the door and the player's mumbled reply doesn't answer the question of who the player is in bed with.

A prominent member, unmarried and handsome, of the Athletics, who must remain nameless here, won a beautiful blonde from strong competition on the overnight lake steamer which carried us from Cleveland to Detroit. His victory was hollow. A few days later he reported ill and spent the next weeks on the bench, never quite recovering from the effects of his one-night romance.

I could have delivered a clubhouse sermon about this tragic curtailment of a promising career if I'd been a manager then. After I became one I did all I could to get ballplayers to marry young. In marriage there's safety from temptation.

Minor injuries didn't concern us as much as they do today's young men. A physician was in attendance at most ball parks, but we usually took our ailments to the trainer. When a player came moaning into the clubhouse the trainer would shrug, "It'll cure itself." Or he'd apply a mixture of wintergreen and vaseline that'd hurt worse than the bruise. Trainers didn't "warm up" a pitcher's arm by pulling it until around 1930. The epidemic of sore arms didn't begin until the slider became popular in the late 1940's. The recent plague of pulled hamstring muscles was unknown to us.

Instead, we got Charley horses, which might mean anything from a twinge of rheumatism to real soreness in the legs. Charley horses caused curses and much gnashing of teeth but they usually cleared up after a few days' lay-off. I suffered a severe Charley horse a little before the 1931 Series. I taped my leg and stayed in the game, perhaps a bit slower but still able to field and run the bases with no noticeable difficulty.

In a game with the Tigers I suffered a spike wound in my left leg. It felt numb as I limped into the clubhouse, but it came to agonizing life as the trainer applied iodine to the wound. Iodine supposedly killed germs. It almost killed me that day. It was a favorite remedy for the "strawberry bruises" incurred from sliding until someone discovered that it irritated exposed tissues.

The club didn't send us to the dentist to have our cavities filled. When a tooth needed capping or extraction we paid the fee ourselves. Nor to an eye specialist to find out if we needed glasses. Not even for an annual physical checkup.

Today's players are treated like fragile china which must be cushioned against shocks. They have diathermy machines, whirlpool baths and other mechanical gadgets around to cure them of anything from halitosis to housemaid's knee. I sometimes wonder if they aren't pampered too much.

I can't remember an old-time pitcher who suffered from the current common sore arm. I'd like to recommend a method of prevention that helped take the soreness out of pitching arms forty-odd years ago.

Every pitcher's arm is sore after pitching half a dozen innings. Many worked out the soreness by bullpen stints between starts. The soreness will disappear totally, however, if the boxman increases the tempo of his throwing during his warm-up for the next game until he is throwing at full speed.

This same energetic kind of practice helped us infielders get in tune for games. We didn't lob the ball around; we fired it; we executed phantom double plays, did cute tricks, won applause from the spectators. It was all part of the show we put on. We got a kick out of practicing. So did our fans.

We played hard, too. The opening game in 1935 was between my White Sox and Mickey Cochrane's Tigers. With the score tied in a late inning I was on third. The batter tapped a slow roller toward first. I took off, hell-bent for scoring the tie-breaking run. Hank Greenberg scooped up the roller, fired underhand to the plate. I slid into Mickey with such force that I bowled him over.

He got up, red-faced, snarling, "I'll get you for this, you son of a sea cook!" He leveled a threatening fist at me. "Don't tell me you're sorry!"

"What could I do? I had to score," I said.

He knew it. . . . I'd have knocked down my grandmother to score that run. Mike was an old pal but this was baseball. I was thirty-nine but I was willing to risk an injury that might have sidelined me forever. Friend-

ship and age never entered my mind. I was playing
for keeps.

We honed our spikes to keep defenders out of our
way when we ran the bases. Ty Cobb never spiked infielders deliberately. When he came sliding in we took
our chances of getting cut. We knew that Ty was determined to touch a piece of the bag before he could be
tagged.

In 1913, when Ty was young and Home Run Baker
was covering third for the Athletics, he and the ball
arrived at the same instant. Baker stood his ground and
put the tag on Ty, who jumped up, fists flying. The
brawl made headlines, and as Baker was Philadelphia's
hero Ty was condemned as a ruffian and a skunk.

"That fight started because I had to let Cobb know
I wasn't afraid of him," Baker told me in afteryears. "I
wore pads under my stockings or I'd have been cut
from ankle to knee."

I was playing second base for the White Sox when
the Tigers' Gee Walker came booming into me to break
up a double play. He grabbed me and tore off every
button off my pants—we didn't wear zippers then. I
called time and told umpire Bill Dinneen, "That bozo
interfered with my throw to first."

"Too bad," said Dinneen. "Have some safety pins
handy the next time he gets on base."

Bucky Harris dished out as good as he got when he
was the Senators' star second sacker. He expected
baserunners to knock him down and he reciprocated
by knocking down whoever covered second when next
he got on base. This was common practice but was no
help when an outfielder got on. We had no way of getting back at him.

I've bowled twenty-five to thirty games many a day during the off-season. It took me a week or two to loosen up my back muscles after I went to camp. But my real love was, and is, golf.

When I was a boy my mother would send me to a nearby farm for a pail of fresh milk. Back of our house was the seventeenth hole of the Merion Cricket Club's links. Golfers lent me clubs and balls and by the time I was ten I was caddying and getting pretty proficient on the fairways. Cochrane, Perkins and Foxx also played golf. Foxx could really comb the ball but he didn't know where it was going, and his putting was poor. I laid off during the 1920's, but came back to the greens in the early '30's and have played ever since.

When Ty Cobb was managing the Tigers he said golf and baseball don't mix. I favored golf as relaxation for my players. Any ballplayer who has the energy to go eighteen holes on the links in his off-time deserves to be encouraged. Golf is better for the legs than sitting around playing cards or fishing. The principles of golf are much the same as in batting: the stance, the grip, the shifting of weight, the breaking of the wrists, the swing, are much the same. The only difference is that the target in golf is stationary whereas it is moving in baseball.

My best round in golf was 63. I celebrated my sixty-ninth birthday with a 69.

So much for Mr. Cobb, who knew more about baseball than any living being but not so much about golf . . .

I hope I've made myself clear about us old-timers. We didn't get bonuses, fees from TV or from personal appearances, and our salaries weren't big enough to start brokerage accounts. We weren't bothered by agents, admen or sponsors. We took the bad with the good and just played baseball, a jolly game, a fun game. Day or night, summer or winter, we had nothing but baseball on our minds.

15

WHO WAS THE GREATEST?

THE HOTTEST question I have to field in my appearances before fan clubs or on the air is: "What was the greatest ball club you've ever seen?" I usually stick out my chin and reply: "The champion Athletics of 1929."

This starts an even hotter argument. Someone inevitably comes back with: "How about the '27 Yankees?"

Well, as Al Smith used to say, "Let's look at the record."

The record shows that the Yankees were murderous ball wallopers. Lou Gehrig led at bat with an impressive .373. Babe Ruth's .356 included his famous sixtieth home run. Earle Combs also hit .356, Bob Meusel had .337, and Tony Lazzeri .309. The Yanks won the pennant by 19 games and crushed the Pirates four straight in the World Series.

For sheer power those Yankees were unequaled. They terrorized pitchers throughout the league. Yet, in my opinion, we '29 Athletics shaded them. We were a better balanced club, with tighter defenses and tighter pitching. I do not say that we were overwhelmingly better. I use the word "shaded" to describe the difference.

Six of us batted over .300—one man more than the five Yankees:

Simmons	.365
Foxx	.354
Miller	.335
Cochrane	.331
Dykes	.327
Haas	.312

I do not say that we could equal the home run punch of Ruth and Gehrig, but I do point out that we were capable of taking command in most games on our hitting alone. The Yankees won 110 games in '27; we won 104 two years later. This difference distributed over a full 154-game season in those one-sided races is slight.

Where we excelled was in fielding. Every man on our club fitted into a stone wall. The line down the middle from Cochrane through Bishop and Boley to Haas in center field has never been matched. Our pivot pair executed double plays with electric speed and artistry. Cochrane was the scrappy holler-guy behind the bat and a masterly handler of pitchers. I can still hear the ball hitting the pitcher's glove as he hurled it back almost as fast as it came in to him, and his cry, "Wake up, guys! Let's give 'em for what! C'mon!" His leadership qualities could be seen, heard, and felt in every game.

I don't want to disparage the pitching of the Yankee starters, Waite Hoyt, Herb Pennock, George Pipgras and Urban Shocker, but they needed the relief pitching of Wilcy Moore to carry them through many games. I classify the tireless pitching of Grove and Earnshaw as more consistent; they fired and fired through more complete games, and we also had Walberg, Rommel, Quinn and Ehmke to back them up.

We had that one great team. The damn Yankees had many. We had challenged them in 1928, tying them for first place on the eve of Labor Day, only to lose the holiday doubleheader and then the pennant, though only by three games. Then came our three great years. I have always maintained that the Athletics quit on themselves in 1932. We had drawn well in '28 and '29 and had played to packed stands in '30, but attendance fell off in '31 and dropped sharply in '32. Empty seats were no inspiration. We saw the beginning of the end and some of us did nothing to put it off. Mr. Mack couldn't pay our high salaries in those days of the Depression. The Yankees finished thirteen games ahead of us. Our day was over. To save his neck he dealt us off.

While we had it we were, although not by a great margin, a slightly better team than that bombing Yankee gang of 1927. That's my firm belief.

I am sometimes asked to name the greatest all-time team, but I decline. I prefer to judge only those teams which I saw from the field of play. One of these was the

Chicago White Sox of 1919, that might-have-been aggregation of super-stars better known as the "Black Sox."

They had a brilliant infield combination in Chick Gandil, Eddie Collins, Carl Risberg and Buck Weaver. Shoeless Joe Jackson led an outfield which had Shano Collins and Happy Felsch beside him. Ray Schalk was behind the bat, catching the shoots of Red Faber, Eddie Cicotte, Claude Williams and Dickie Kerr. They played in what's since been called the dead-ball era, but Jackson's .351, Collins' .319, Weaver's .296 and Gandil's .290 supplied plenty of punch.

I didn't play much against them in 1919 but I saw them roll over their opposition. Came fall, and the sellout of some of them in the World Series was a great shock to us all. I don't condone it but I'd like to point out that the temptation was great—the highest salary on the team was less than $10,000.

The story of baseball might well have been different if that fine team had not been broken up as the result of tampering by gamblers.

Now let me take another dive into hot water by naming a few all-star teams. I'm confining my selections to the American League, for I saw little National League play.

My all-stars of the 1920's have Gehrig at first base. He outslugged Foxx by a small margin. His fielding was criticized during his early years but he became an adequate first sacker later, handling the bag well, grabbing difficult chances. As a slugger he was power-plus.

At second I rate Charlie Gehringer best. Charlie was like a mechanical man in the field, as smart as Lazzeri, as much a perfectionist as Boley—and his lifetime batting average was .321. He was still at his peak as the decade ended, still getting everything that came his way and coming through with much more than his share of bingles.

Teamed with Gehringer, at short must be that other marvel of consistent play, Everett Scott. Scotty moved from the Red Sox to the Yankees in 1922 when he was in the midst of an eight-year streak of consecutive games. During this period he also led the league in fielding averages for shortstops for eight seasons, a remarkable record which stands unequaled in today's record books. Scott was a master in the game's most vital position. His modest stickwork was outweighed by his teammates' Bronx Bombing. He was a vital cog in those Yankee pennant drives.

At third I raise my cap to Jumping Joe Dugan, who could outjump, outget and outthrow any one of us and all. Joe played on the Athletics with me until 1922 when he was traded to the Red Sox, and finally to New York, where he spent his best years. He also had good offensive power, hitting around .290 for the decade.

Picking the outfield is easy. In left Ty Cobb, who knew every possible trick in the book that'd get him on and then show some new ones to us who got in his way. No one has yet surpassed Ty as a hitter and baserunner and no one ever will.

In center is another genius of those days, Tris Speaker, who wound up his years in the majors beside Ty on the 1928 Athletics. I saw the last flashes of Spoke's greatness. To me he was the model outfielder, graceful, deadly in running down tough flies and with a perfect sense of timing at bat.

In right, of course, Babe Ruth. 'Nuff said.

My catcher is Mickey Cochrane. I've already talked enough about him.

I don't put Walter Johnson on my squad for sentimental reasons. He ended his career in '27 and had lost some of his smoke by the time I got into the batting groove. I thank my stars I didn't have to face him when he was in his prime.

My southpaw starter can only be Lefty Grove. His won-lost percentage was higher than any other Hall of Famer. He was the greatest of the left-handers, Sandy Koufax included. His intense desire to win made him the perfect starter in any crucial game.

Among other lefties who stand out in my memory is Herb Pennock. Herb had a fine fast ball, an overhand curve difficult to meet solidly and that eyelash control which he depended on after his fast one went. Herb was cool, crafty, mixed brains with his deliveries and stood out there daring the best batters of the day to hit him.

Some team, eh?

Now let's look at the players of the 1930 to 1941 period. There can be no doubt that the Yankees of 1936–1941 rank as one of the great all-time teams. They won five of six pennants, missing the 1940 flag by two games. They were not as powerful as the '27 Yanks or as our Athletic champions, but they were brilliant on defense and loaded with first-line pitching.

Turning to the all-star team of prewar years I award first base to Jimmy Foxx, whose slugging continued throughout the period. Jimmy came closest to Ruth's 60 home runs with 58 in 1932. He clouted more than 30 homers in every year in the 30's. Put him up there, second only to the Babe.

Gehringer remains at second. His fielding was as steady as ever. Only once did he fail to hit .300 or more. His .371 topped the league in '37.

Luke Appling, my old buddy, was the league's greatest shortstop during those years. Luke made all the plays, had a strong arm that got runners at first base from the deepest hole. Like Gehringer he hit over .300 in all years but one. His phenomenal .388 was highest in '38, when he was at his peak.

Red Rolfe, the brainy Yankee, was a professor of position play at third. He speared drives to his left and along the foul line, his pickups of bunts were beautiful. Red was also an expert baserunner although not fast. His knowledge of outfielders' handling of ground-ball singles enabled him to stretch many into two-base hits. He was an ideal No. 2 batter, smart on the hit-and-run. Four times he batted over .300.

In 1930 and 1931 Al Simmons led the American League with .381 and .390. He was up over .300 every year until 1935. He was the greatest right-hand hitter of his day and a better than average outfielder. I shift him to right field to make room in left for young Ted Williams.

Ted gets into the all-star lineup on his two great years, 1940 and 1941. As a rookie he hit .344, as a second-year man a magic .406. This alone gives him the right to all-star honors. His judgment of pitching, his accurate swing, his power were all in one piece in his rookie years. Call him unmatchable.

Mickey Cochrane's only competitor for the all-star catching job is Bill Dickey, as smooth a receiver as I've ever seen. Bill was at his hitting best before the war. Between Mickey and Bill there's little to choose in pitcher handling. Bill's calmness suited McCarthy's

Yankees; Mike's fire heated the Athletics and made the Tigers roaring hot. Bill deserves recognition—put his name on the lineup card.

It's Bob Feller all the way as my right-hand starter. Bob added a great curve to his terrifying speed about 1939, his fourth year in the majors. The combination made him the toughest right-hander to hit.

And for lefties it's still Grove.

I don't like to say "the good old times" were over when the war began but it's true . . . the game has changed since peace came and not always for the better. The Dodgers of the 1947–1955 period most nearly compare with our champion Athletics and the '27 Yanks. They won six pennants in ten years. They had power in Duke Snider, Gil Hodges, Roy Campanella and Jackie Robinson, and a fine defense in Jackie, Pee Wee Reese, Billy Cox and Carl Furillo, while the pitching of Preacher Roe, Carl Erskine and Johnny Podres can't be sneezed at.

But sticking to the American League, it has to be those Yankees again. They also dominate the postwar all-star lineup.

Not at first base, however. My choice is Joe Kuhel, whose career was almost over as the war ended. Joe was no Jimmy Foxx or Lou Gehrig with the stick, but he was a better-than-average hitter for seventeen seasons. He was the best-fielding first sacker I've ever seen. He was fast and smart on the bases, he could steal and get the extra base. He could do all the things expected of a winning ballplayer. He belongs up there with the all-stars.

Bobby Richardson is my second baseman; Bobby hit with the pitch in the old-fashioned way. He was a ballplayer who knew all the answers, steady, steadier, steadiest. He knew how to play position and played it so well he led the league in double plays for a second sacker in five seasons. He was fast on the bases, the kind of infielder I like.

Alongside Bobby at shortstop is that little bundle of pep, Phil Rizzuto, a hitter with more power than seemed possible for a man of his size, a master of the bunt, a weapon that's been neglected of late. He covered short with the best of 'em. He was lightning fast on the bases. Hitting, fielding, running—what more can you ask?

Brooks Robinson is at third, a lad with quick reflexes, with the ability to leap into the pitch with power, a strong clutch hitter, a top RBI man. He covers his territory as if he owned every inch of it, handles bunts with the greatest of ease. A very good ballplayer . . .

Ted Williams stays on in left field. Four batting titles in the postwar years, one at .383 when he was 39 . . . the most dangerous hitter of his day.

Picking a center fielder is complicated. I'm exercising the manager's option by shifting Mickey Mantle from center to right field in order to make room for Joe DiMaggio, whose place he took in the Yankee garden. I'd really like to have two DiMaggios on my team, Joe and Dom. Dom was a better center fielder in my book than Brother Joe. He got a quicker jump on the ball and covered more ground. As a hitter he stroked at a .298 clip. But Joe's superiority at bat can't be denied. And I don't remember his making a poor play in the field.

Then, in right, Mantle. If Mickey's legs had stayed healthy he'd be up there with Ruth, Cobb, Speaker and

Foxx. What power! What speed! And a switch-hitter, too . . .

And here's another Yankee behind the bat, Yogi Berra, who rates with Cochrane and Dickey as a handler of pitchers. Yogi was best in the clutch, a late-inning game-buster, a rough hitter, as I well know. No American League catcher of the past twenty years was in a class with the guy.

And more Yankees . . . Allie Reynolds and Whitey Ford. Allie had a blazing strikeout fast ball in his Cleveland years. He was wise in mastering a fine curve and mixing it well with his speed after he joined the Yanks in '47. By '52 he led the league in earned run averages and pitched two no-hitters. He's clearly the best right-hander since the war.

Ford is at the head of the southpaw class. He delivered the ball where and how he wanted to, with various speeds and curves. I call him the pitcher with the know-how, the brainy kind. He came through with wins in crucial games. His winning record was over .700. A smart cookie, this Ford . . .

16

WELL, THERE YOU HAVE IT . . .

Yes, that's it, my fifty years in baseball. As I said when we sat down, I've seen and talked to 'em all, and I've been pitted against most of 'em, either playing my fool head off or managing boys who were.

There's nothing better than being in baseball. It's like joining an exclusive club. It's getting the best education money can buy, an education in life. It's being somebody and giving pleasure to others while being somebody.

It's not all ups. It's hard work, but who's afraid of hard work? It's much easier today than back when I was a boy. We did it ourselves. Nowadays there are coaches,

217

teachers, fine equipment, and bonus checks, a guaranteed minimum wage, high pay if you make good, honors when you win, and a substantial pension when you're through.

And, on the side, lifelong friendships, good fellowship, fun. And wonderful memories . . .

Right now there's a shortage of players. Opportunities are open to any kid who can hit, run, throw. Maybe you can. Maybe you know some kid who can. The more the merrier, the better baseball will be. If I've made you understand what it's like to spend your life in baseball I've said my piece for today.

So put it there, pal. Nice to have talked to you. Have fun . . .